# The Streets Will Never Close 2

**Lock Down Publications and**
**Ca$h**
**Presents**

# The Streets Will Never Close 2

**A Novel by *K'ajji***

**Lock Down Publications**
P.O. Box 944
Stockbridge, Ga 30281
www.lockdownpublications.com


First Edition February 2022
Printed in the United States of America



**Lock Down Publications**
**Like our page on Facebook: Lock Down Publications @**
**www.facebook.com/lockdownpublications.ldp**
Book interior design by: **Shawn Walker**
Edited by: **Lashonda Johnson**

**Stay Connected with Us!**

Text **LOCKDOWN** to 22828 to stay up-to-date with new releases, sneak peaks, contests and more…

Thank you!

**Submission Guideline.**

Submit the first three chapters of your completed manuscript to ldpsubmissions@gmail.com, subject line: Your book's title. The manuscript must be in a .doc file and sent as an attachment. Document should be in Times New Roman, double spaced and in size 12 font. Also, provide your synopsis and full contact information. If sending multiple submissions, they must each be in a separate email.

Have a story but no way to send it electronically? You can still submit to LDP/Ca$h Presents. Send in the first three chapters, written or typed, of your completed manuscript to:

LDP: Submissions Dept
P.O. Box 944
Stockbridge, Ga 30281

*DO NOT send original manuscript. Must be a duplicate.*

Provide your synopsis and a cover letter containing your full contact information.

Thanks for considering LDP and Ca$h Presents.

If you're a BAD B*TCH and you know it, join the PYT CHALLENGE for your chance to WIN A CASH PRIZE!!!!! Enter by uploading your Photos, Snapchat, or live videos to Google Drive. Share them with K'AJJI @PYT1986TSWNC@gmail.com. Reenact your favorite scene, or simply REPRESENT where you're from. PLEASE USE CAUTION.

You may also send comments on your favorite characters to the author directly by writing:

Davion Davis #432095
Redgranite Correctional Institution
PO BOX 189
Phoenix, MD 21131

# Chapter 1

## *LUE*

### *5:00 A.M. Present Day*

"Sweets! Sweeetttsss! Bitch, I'ma kill youuu!" She tossed and turned, yelling and actually cried in her sleep. All the while, she clutched her .45s.

"Hood! Hood, get up! You trippin'!" Mula yelled, shaking her awake.

Startled, she woke up to see all of us standing around her, staring.

Breathless and feeling woozy, she sat up pointing her weapons. "Where she—where they at!" Her chest was rising and falling at a fast pace.

"Whoa! Hood, you alright! You a'ight!" Bri assured.

Realizing it was just us, she lowered her guns. Mula wiped her tears away.

Sweets said, "Damn, you gon' kill me, huh? What I do?"

Hood jumped up off the couch. "Kaaarm! Oh, my God!" She grabbed her and hugged her, tears making trails down her face.

"Sweets! Ohhhh!" she cried. "I wasn't talkin' about chuuuu! Not youuu!" She held her close.

"Dang, Hood! Y—you squeezin' me too tight. What's wrong?" she asked in confusion.

"I-I-had a—"

"Bad dream?" I questioned.

"A nightmare. Let me look at youuu! Girrrl!" She grasped Karma's shoulders, looked her over and hugged her again. "I just had this crazy ass dream! They shot chu!"

"Who!" Mula questioned.

"The Po—lice!" Hood replied.

"Damn, did I die?" Sweets asked with a bit of concern in her voice.

She's always been big on dreams. She believes they all mean something one way or another. No response from Hood had her upset.

Hood broke their embrace and rushed over to the window, just as she'd done in her dream. She said, "It was just a dream, Sweets." She peered through the blinds.

"So, what bitch! I wanna know! Did-I-die!"

Hood didn't wanna tell her. But she walked back over to her and looked her directly in her eyes.

"Ye—yeah! Yeah, alright! Is that what you wanted to hear? You died! And we was fucked up! It was that bitch Burke an-and a-a muthafuckin' SWAT team." Hood spoke with her hands as she paced back and forth.

We all gasped. Sweets had to sit down after hearing that shit. I sat next to her and hugged her.

"Where was we at?" Mula asked, hands on her hips.

Hood ran her fingers through her hair in thought. "Here," she replied. "What happened last night anyways?"

I said, "Damn! Were you that fucked up that you don't even remember?"

She paused and looked at me. "You was telling us about you, Moo, Doe and Teague. We was still gettin' our drink and our smoke on, when yo' ass fell asleep."

Bri said, "Yeah, and you know the rules. Being you were the first to go, we started to whip up some of that mystery potion and put some on your lips." She laughed, trying to break the tension in the air. "You lucky we ain't wanna mess up this pretty carpet of yours."

It's just a little game we'd play, where we take every condiment we can find from the kitchen to the medicine cabinet. We'd mix it all together like a smoothie. So, you had toothpaste, Hot Sauce, mustard, ketchup, Barbecue sauce and all kinds of shit. When we'd vow to pull an *all-nighter*, the first one of us that fell asleep got it. We'd put it in ya hair, on your hands and your face. Wherever-the-fuck-ever. Usually, the victim woke up mad—as—hell!

Hood said, “Nah, y’all lucky. I would’ve beat that ass!” She smiled. “I’ma go take care of my shit, then make breakfast. Who hungry?” She could see Sweets was still visibly upset.

While the rest of us were giving our requisitions to what we wanted for breakfast she hadn’t said a word.

Hood attempted to comfort her as she walked past. “Sweets, you ain’t gotta worry about that shit. It ain’t gon’ happen. My dreams don’t tend to come true. Just forget-about-it. A’ight?”

Though Hood didn’t want any of us to notice, she was still affected by the dream as well.

## Chapter 2

### *BRI*

*Hmmm! About time! She got some gourmet cookin' goin' on up in here!* I thought catching a whiff of the aroma in the air as I stepped out of the bathroom.

It was so invigorating that my mouth started waterin'. I'm hungry, too! The smell of sausage links and bacon led me straight to her. I walked up behind her as she stood in the kitchen over the stove flipping pancakes.

"Hood, Cyn called while you were in the shower. She said she wants a plate. Plus, she wanna know if you'd be down to go to Racine tonight?" She turned toward me wearing a frown.

"I know. Lue told me. I guess I'll think about it."

She shook her head. "Cyn get on my damn nerves. Here she go tryin' to run up behind Money's sorry ass again. Can't she talk them fools into coming up here?"

"I don't know," I replied. "We can discuss it when she gets here. She on her way. What up with you, though? You good?"

"Yeah, I'm a'ight. Ever since we hit them Bag Niggaz, I've been having these crazy ass dreams."

"Oh, really? Is that what got you sleeping with your finger on the trigger?" Sweets asked, overhearing the conversation as she'd walked into the kitchen.

Hood said, "Look, Sweets, to be honest the dreams never even went that far. I guess seeing that Police-bitch on the news talkin' that vigilante shit got to me. Don't trip."

"Uh-huh! Easy for you to say," Sweets replied, reaching around her, snatching a piece of cooling bacon off the stove and stuffing it in her mouth.

Hood said, "You ain't gotta be sneakin'. The rest of the food is in the oven. Make you a plate. Matter fact, just sit-down. I'll make 'em. Lue and Mula! Y'all come and eat!" she yelled.

"So, where did I leave off last night?" she questioned as we gathered around the kitchen table. We took our seats.

I said, "At the old steel mill off Capitol."

"Chop-cha—oppp!" She laughed. "I know y'all remember hearing about that shit? That night, J.L.'s bitch-ass paid for his treachery with his life. Carving him up in slabs, we stuffed the body parts in black garbage bags. After throwing him in the trunk, we burnt the mill to the ground. I remember glancing back at the sweltering blaze as if it were yesterday as we cruised up the block.

*Teague telling me, "Don't look back baby girl. Never look back." He patted my thigh. "It's over."*

She said, "Some say death is always hard on the living. It may be true in some cases, but not his. His death ain't hard on me at all. He took my mother away from me. Fuck 'em. I don't feel guilty."

I said, "So, you were there when they—you know?"

I raised my eyebrows inquisitively. I didn't want to spoil anybody's appetite, but I had to know.

"What? When they posted him on the block?"

I nodded, as I grabbed the plate, she was handing me. She'd nodded and smiled, but she was just fuckin' with me.

She said, "Nah. Nuh-un, though I should've been. They'd dropped me off. I heard about it on the news, just like y'all did."

I let out a sigh of relief.

# PART 1

## *The Book of John*

# Chapter 3

*"Breaking News, just as we come on the air this morning and reports come in. A trail of carnage on Milwaukee's Northside leaves early commuters stunned as authorities search for clues. Tony is live on the scene—"*

## *GINA*

An overflow of calls was coming in from one area. Barreling down Burleigh at one hundred miles per hour, I came to a stop, jumping out in the middle of the ghetto. I was immediately swarmed by reporters as officers taped off the scene.

"Detective! Detective Burke! I'm Tony Loton with TMJ 4! Can you tell us—" A sequence of cameras flashed taking my picture.

"I don't give a damn who you're with! Now move! Get them damn cameras outta my face! Move! Get back goddamnit! Let me through!"

There was a moment's pause before they parted like the Red Sea.

The buzz of blow flies and the distinct prate of onlookers only enhanced the enigmatic horror before me as I ducked under the tape. Whomever committed this heinous act had to be heartless. This was some medieval shit here!

"Either get them kids in the house or gone take 'em to school!" I yelled, shewing the crowd of spectators. "They shouldn't be seein' this!"

"Officer! You! Yeah, you! Come here!" He walked over to me nervously.

"Get everybody back! You're on the job. Don't just be just standing out here lookin' crazy! Make sure you get some other officers and y'all clear it out! Then I want y'all to canvass the area. Everybody, get back! Babies don't look!" I cringed with a frown. "Gone! Get to it. Whatcha waiting on?"

The new boot finally moved to do as he was told. I'm looking up at the decapitated head of a black male. Somebody mounted it on a pole at the corner of 24th where the stop sign is usually displayed. Sweeping through like a plague, the morning air reeks of rotting flesh. Covering my mouth and my nose with my right hand, I move in for a closer look. The blood on his face seemed fresh, enhaloed by the sun, but the lack of it seemed to mean that the head was severed elsewhere. The mutilation caused swelling, so his features are mushy. I don't recognize him. There seems to be something carved in his forehead. A word. Squinting, I shade my eyes with my other hand, but I can't make it out due to the daystar's powerful glare. Searching the immediate area, I found nothing.

Ten minutes later, the Forensic Team rolled in and got out. They were dressed for the occasion, in all white coveralls and masks. Stepping back to get out of their way, I can't run from the wretched odor and its range. I'm starting to feel a bit dizzy.

"Whew! I'm so glad y'all made it. Get on in there! Dig it up carefully. We don't want it poppin' up off there now! Take the entire pole," I directed.

One hand resting on the holstered Beretta on my hip, I walked back toward my car. Surveying the area, I've got a clear view of the poverty—stricken old wooden and brick houses and the unkept yards. I glanced at the faces of my captive audience, young and old. Amongst the crowd captured by this domineering act of violence an infant's cry is swallowed by the deafening wails of sirens as units race up Chambers heading westbound. Suddenly, the radio chatter grew immensely. Leaning in, I grabbed my transmitter off the passenger seat, seeing the big fella in motion.

"Jamison, whatcha got? Talk to me," I chimed in.

"We've got a torso up the block from you on fortieth in Burleigh! But that's not all! There's thighs, calves, forearms and other parts throughout the neighborhood! Somebody really slaughtered this guy!" he came back.

"What! Are you serious? Who would do some shit like this, knowing all these babies are on their way to school!"

"I don't know, but it's like a meat market out here. How you doing on that end? Anything on the canvass?"

"Nope, not yet! And it's pretty bad. Yo' ass bet not touch nothin'! Just see if there is anything significant we can use. I'm talking scars, jewelry on the hands take it if you find some. Any tattoos?"

"It's funny you should ask."

"What? What is it?"

"Our victim actually had some ink work done. Though I'm just getting here, I can tell you this much. Seems distinguishable enough."

"What is it of?"

"There's a tat that reads Cuppy Love across the abdomen," he replied.

*Wait a minute,* I thought, looking back at the head being carefully placed in a evidence's bag. My heart dropped instantaneously. I hit the transmitter button. "Come again?"

"We've got a tattoo across the stomach area that says Cuppy Love. Cee, as in cat. U, as in upper. Pee, as in Peter. There's two of those. And Y, as in you. Love. L-O-V-E! Mean anything to you?" he asked.

Dropping my head in pain before responding, I said, "Yeah. Yes, it does. I know who our victim is, assuming all these parts came from one individual. I've been trying to get him for years. You wouldn't believe it."

"Well, who? We won't know what I'll believe until you tell me what it is you're thinking.

"It's Mr. LeVon."

"The dealer? Are you certain? I mean, isn't this supposed to be his land?

"Yup, I'm positive. Booked him enough times to know. That ink is well documented in my file. There's no other tat like it in the federal database. He musta really pissed somebody off. I just need to wrap things up here, then I'm on my way to you. Give me about thirty minutes."

"Copy that."

I'm hurt. Not for him, but for someone else that I love dearly. I knew John to be responsible for dozens of murders, as well as the heavy drug distribution in this community and others. I'd always hoped I'd be the one to take that ass down. Shit, though I wanted him out of her life and had cursed him dead on many occasions, in my heart I felt different for her sake. I now wondered how somebody managed to not only invade his territory; but to leave such a hideous message behind? The word *GREED* had been scribed across his forehead in all caps.

# Chapter 4

## *FATIMA*

So much for sleeping good. Hell, I'm up now. The heat generating from my queen size waterbed is so soothing against my nakedness, I don't wanna move! But the damn phone was ringing off the hook. Rolling over, I reached through the sheer white canopy toward the nightstand.

"Ugh! All right! Alright, damn!" I picked up. "Hello! Oh, hey Lex." It's my best friend Alexus. "Hm? Wh-what time is it?" I yawned. "You called how many times? Girrl, I went out last night. You know I really don't drink so. What!" I sat up. "When!" I gasped as her words sat in on my stomach. "Bitch, don't play. You lyin'. Who told you that? When? I-I just—I was just with him last night! Naw! Hell naw."

I slid outta bed, throwing on my red negligee. "Have you talked to Congo or Spree? I'm, I am! Let me pack a bag. I know Lex! Lemme, let me call you back!" Hanging up the phone, I picked up the remote and turned on the TV.

Glancing at the clock, it read 11:15 A.M. The news wouldn't be back on for another forty-five minutes. I rushed into the closet, grabbed my emergency suitcase, and ran it to the foyer. Then, I booked it back to the room and got my duffel bag. With my head spinning out of control, I dialed his number as I slipped in my jeans and threw on a sweater. I grabbed the bag and hurried out of the master bedroom heading for the den. Hearing the rumbling thunder as rain pelted off the windows amplified the thousands of bone chilling images running through my mind.

"Come on Jay! Answer this damn phone!" I screamed as tears brimmed my eyelids causing a sting.

The line at the mansion just rung. Hanging up, I paged him. He always called me right' back. I sat the phone down on the floor next to me. My body twitched and my hands trembled a I struggled with the combination to the safe in the den under his desk. If what Lex said is true, whoever got to him could easily be on their way to snatch me up next. I'm not sticking around to find out.

Cracking the safe, I emptied it of its contents. Money, important documents, as well as his black book containing the plug's info and everybody that worked for him. I'd already collected the majority of the cash, though there was some out there I hadn't gotten to. That was my job when he was out of town on business. I've got about 1.2 million, plus the few hundred thousand in my account.

Opening the drawer to the desk, I grabbed the Taurus and two boxes of shells. Just as I was about to drop the .9mm in the bag, the doorbell rang. Walking over to the windows, I look, but don't see anybody. Whoever was out there had parked in front of the house, instead of alongside the curb where the den is located. Loving J.L. came with consequences and some more shit. Avarice, his wife don't play. But I refused to lose just like she did. Me and him had an agreement. I'd respect her slot, as long as we could share. She didn't like it, but he'd pursued me! I'd come a long way from dancing for dollars at Ricky's. I don't plan on going back. I knew I was chancing death, but I ain't ready to die. I got his gun, cocked it, and made my way to the front door.

"Who is it!" I yelled. I heard a female's voice, but I couldn't tell what she'd said. "Who!" stepping to side, I peeked through the curtain.

I damn sure wasn't about to put my eye to the peephole. If it is Cuppy she got me fucked up.

It wasn't her, though. It was some lady that look like Taraji P, but she was the muthafuckin' police. I crept back a few feet and slid the gun in drawer of the table where we usually kept the mail. I opened the door drying my face of tears with my sleeve.

She said, "Hi. Hate to bother you. My name is Gina. I'm with MPD, Homicide. I was expecting Mrs. LeVon." She tried looking past me. "Clearly you're not her. Is she home?"

"No, she doesn't live here. Well, not anymore."

"And you are?" She looked stunned.

"I'm Fatima. Fatima Cage."

"Ms. Cage, do mind if I ask your relation to Mr. LeVon?"

"I'm a friend."

"In friend, do you mean mistress or—"

"Y-yeah, I guess you can say that." I nodded.

She rolled her eyes, sighed heavily and crossed her arms. "Right. When they're married, that's usually what that means. Is there anyone else home?" She had this impious attitude.

"No there's not, I'm alone," I replied.

"It's wet out here. Do you mind if I come in? I have some terrible news. I'd also like to ask you a few questions."

"No, I don't mind. Please come in." Stepping aside, I let her in.

As she stepped over the threshold, I saw her eyes shifting checking her surroundings. I closed the door and stepped around her leading her into the living room.

"Follow me," I told her.

"You pulling up stakes?"

"Excuse me?" I glanced back. She was on my heels.

"The suitcase. It looks as if you're about to take a trip."

"Oh, I'm just heading to a friend's."

"Would that be a male or female?" she asked.

"My friend Alexus Waters. She's female. Please." I gestured for her to have a seat.

"Nall, you gon' head. I'll stand, thanks. Ms. Cage, you seem a little jumpy. Do you know why I'm here?" her voice said it all.

Nervously, I moved a throw pillow and placed it in my lap as I took a seat on the chocolate leather sofa. Everything I was thinking and feeling suddenly came out.

"I was sleep. I—I got a phone call and now you're here. I'm hoping that—"

"He's still alive?" she asked. I just nodded.

My tears were now flowing excessively.

"He's gone, Ms. Cage, I'm sorry."

"N—o—o-o-o-o! What am I gonna do!" I cried. "I'm only twenty-three! I don't have nobodyyyy!" Bringing the pillow to my face, I screamed.

The officer patted my back. "It's gon' be alright. I need you to stay calm as you can for me, okay. When was the last time you saw him?"

"Last night!" I bawled.

"I was told he was seen accompanied by a young woman at People's down on Burleigh last night. Were you with him? Was that you?"

"Yeah, that was me. After we left there, we went to his house out on Lake Drive! Sh—she sa-said she wa-was gone kill us if she ever caught us together again," I cried.

"Who? Who are you referring to?" she asked.

"His wife! It's his wife! I know it was! She gone kill meee!"

"Wait a minute. You were at his house on Lake Drive last night?"

I nodded.

"And what happened? Did his wife show up?"

"I don't knowww! We were in the bed, an—and the doorbell rang." I swallowed hard, trying to compose myself.

"Okay. The doorbell rang. Who was it?"

"I couldn't tell you. He got up to answer it, and he never came back. He didn't come baaack! My car was outside! I was so scared. She was supposed to be in Jamaicaaa!"

"Is there anyone else you can think of that would want to hurt Mr. LeVon?" she asked. I shook my head. She said, "Cause I don't think his wife is capable of this. Not the way we found him."

"It was her," I replied in a voice that was low and uneven.

She said, "I'll look into it. I'm sorry but being you're the last person to see him alive I'm gonna need you to come down to the station so we can fill out a report."

"Okay." I nodded. "I'll come with you. Do you mind dropping me off at my friend's after we're done?"

"No, not at all."

"I—I can't drive now. It's—"

"I understand. No need to explain. Just grab your things. I'll take you. It's no problem.

# Chapter 5

## *GINA*

Fatima was young, dark skinned and very pretty. She had high cheekbones, solemn eyes and long, straight, black hair. Her features were well defined. She had an African queen glow about her. I could see why many men would fall victim to her web. Let alone John and what was his old-soured age. Her butt sat high on her frame, long legged, her breasts were still perky.

This in which told me she either was yet to carry a child, or her workout game was stupid. I took her absence in gathering her things as an opportunity to be nosy. The house is immaculately neat. Not a speck of dust in sight. High ceilings, silk curtains, expensive China and extravagant furniture from God knows where. One could never assume that she was just another bum bitch living a frugal lifestyle. There was also the Mercedes parked out in the driveway.

"Ahem—excuse you! What exactly do you think you're doing?" she asked, looking at me questionably. "You lookin' for somethin'?"

I was caught in the act, snooping. She'd snuck up behind me. I was all the way upstairs.

"Oh, I'm sorry. I was just lookin' around. This is such a nice place. I hope you don't mind. I had to make sure you didn't have nobody up in here hiding." I gave her a smile.

She pursed her lips to the side, giving me that face that said she didn't believe me. "Well, I do mind. Ain't nobody up here! Can we get outta here and gon' get this over with?"

"Look, girl, don't be gettin' all overly optimistic with me! I was waitin' on you."

"Well, I'm ready!" she replied in a tone that was a little too husky for my taste.

But I was in her home, so I didn't argue. I took a deep breath, holding my tongue. I was satisfied that she wasn't hiding anybody. She followed me closely down the spacious hallway leading back downstairs. I counted two more bags next to the one she'd sat at the front door.

"Need some help with those?" I asked as we descended down the staircase.

"Nall, I think I'll manage."

I shrugged. "Suit yourself." I wouldn't ask her ass no more.

Outside the rain had started to dance a little drizzle. As we were walking up the walkway, I paused. I noticed that same gray SUV idling at the end of the block, just as it had been when I'd arrived. Though distant, I could see two mysterious figures tucked inside. I found this strange, knowing not too many people of my skin color resided out here in Brown Deer.

"What you doin'? You gon' pop the trunk or what?" Fatima asked, bringing me out of the trance caused by the mixture of the quiet calm rain, the smog rising from the trucks loud dual pipes and it's squeaky windshield wipers. Looking back, she had two of her bags in tow.

"Oh, yeah." I gave her a dismissive wave. *Am I trippin'?* I thought. *Hell nah!* I answered in my mind. "Damn, what you bringing, the whole house? Those bags lookin' real heavy."

She was clearly struggling with them. "Nah, just a few things." She sniffled.

"Give me a sec. I'll have to move a few things, then you can throw those in." I walked around my car, got in and popped the trunk.

Checking my rearview mirror on the door as I opened it, I saw that the occupants in the truck hadn't budged. Yeah, something was definitely up. I got out and quickly maneuvered toward the trunk. Grabbing my vest from inside, I threw it over my head and strapped it to my chest.

"Ms. Cage—do me a favor."

"What?"

"Put the bags down and step over here. Come on, hurry up!"

"What's wrong?" she asked, hearing the urgency in my voice.

"I want you to take a look at that truck behind us."

She froze. "Is som-somebody—"

"Listen to me. Don't panic. Just look. The gray one at the corner. You recognize it?"

She glanced over her shoulder as I grabbed my VR 60 semi-automatic shotgun. There was no time to call for backup. She'd have to do.

"Nall," she replied. "I ain't never seen it before.

"I didn't think so. Leave the luggage right there and go back inside," I told her calmly and collective as I could.

"But I—"

"Now!" I slammed the trunk shut.

Wearing a shaken expression, she ran back in the house. I jacked the slide, and cautiously headed in the direction of the vehicle. I heard the truck's gears shift as I approached. Taking aim, I picked up the pace. Now, I'm running toward them as the rubber on the truck's rear end spun in reverse on the wet pavement.

"Stop! Police!" I commanded, as the driver whipped the truck around, narrowly missing a parked car.

His passenger raised his pistol, but the driver grabbed his arm.

"Freeezeee! Stop the truck!" I shouted with authority to no avail.

Throwing it in drive, the tires screeched, and they careened up the roadway leaving me in the middle of the street smelling the exhaust.

*Fuck!* They'd gotten away.

Fatima came running out as I neared her home.

"Girl! What you gotcha self into! That damn sure wasn't his wife! They weren't selling Girl Scout cookies or stopping by to see how you were doing either! I saw a gun! Who was that!"

"I-I don't know!" she whined.

I called in the description of the truck, but I knew they were long gone.

"Well, you gon' have to tell me something more than, *"you don't know."* Yo' ass know somethin'! Getcha shit and let's go."

I had her ass right where I wanted her. In the Hot Seat. The more she explained, the more I began to hate I'd even asked. What she said changed everything. While she may be right about John's wife wanting her out of the way, all the money she had access to was a cause for concern as well.

# Chapter 6

## *PO*

In reminiscence of our past, we tried to balance it out. Bullets and money. I remember being eager to cross paths with this nigga. I'd heard about his hold on The Zoo long before I met him. Though I hate to admit it, my reminiscence intentions weren't good. Nah, the way I saw it back then, hittin' him meant I could lean all the way back for a minute. Maybe even retire from all this lawlessness. Shit, I was street dreaming, but things didn't go as planned. We happened to bump into each other one Friday night. See, J.L. got his nose dirty from time to time. Rumor had it, he loved getting fucked up and trickin' on the hoes.

I found what I thought might of been some truth to it, listening to this stripper Tion tell her buddy he'd be attending the shindig she was throwing and that he always brought plenty of paper. At first, I thought she was just blowing smoke. I'd fucked Tion's lying ass a few times. Though she was a bad bitch physically, her crib stayed nasty. I found it hard to believe a nigga of J.L.'s caliber would be caught dead out in Westlawn with her, her bad ass kids and all them roaches. I got tired of shaking my shit out like a rug every time I left that mufucka. I vowed to never return, but I couldn't miss out on the opportunity to hit this lick.

Shockingly, when I crept off in that joint in the middle of the night, there he was. *He slippin'! I gotta have this nigga! I want everything he got!* I thought as he sat at the living room table with Tion and another bitch sitting on his lap feeding his nostrils with cocaine. I was trying to stay low, using the darkness of the living room and the black hoodie I had on to obscure my identity. But my nigga, T-Weezy was sitting at the table. He'd spotted me lurking.

"Lil Folks!" he yelled over the music.

I kept it moving, maneuvering through the confined space as if I didn't hear him. It was just my luck that the song was coming to its ending. Tion musta looked up and caught me trying to escape.

"Po! Po' Kelly, where you goin' boy!" she yelled.

I paused. What I do that for? Not wanting to seem too suspicious, I turned around and strolled over to the table where they were seated. Surprisedly, though we'd never met, J.L. was the first to speak.

"So, you the lil nigga that's been terrorizing the city?" he sized me up wearing a smug expression. Downing his drink, he smiled. "I thought you'd be ten feet tall and weigh eight-hundred pounds? As many niggaz you done robbed and all the guns you done bussed around this muthafucka!"

I said, "Nah, this me nigga. God in the flesh."

"God?" He shook his head. "How old are you, little nigga?"

"Seventeen, why?"

He said, "God can't die, so you ain't Him. You know you can't continue to live this life you lead without heading to prison or worse, an early grave don't cha?"

I just stared. He told Tion, "Give daddy another hit, baby."

She lifted the plate, placed the rolled up hundred-dollar bill to his nostril and he snorted another line.

"I got something for you." He looked up at me. "Here." He handed me his business card and asked that I give him a call in the morning.

Turned out the nigga wasn't dumb as I thought. He had Spree and Congo watching my every move. Though I still wanted to hit 'em, I had to turn the killa instinct down a few notches. He knew his come up made him a target, and it wouldn't be long before me, or a nigga just like me came for his cash and his brains. He'd later reveal my weakness. He told me my eyes couldn't hide my true intentions for him. I guess I've always worn my hunger like clothing.

Anyway, I hollered at Weezy for a minute, then got up outta there. When I hit J.L. the next day, he asked that I meet him at a spot he'd just opened out on Hampton in the projects. When I got there, he asked his goons to step outside before throwing a duffel bag at my feet. Taking a puff of his Cuban cigar, he reclined in his chair.

"You should come work for me as one of my guns," he suggested.

"Your guns? Fuck you talkin' about?" I looked down at the bag at my feet, then back up at him.

I couldn't believe this Blair Underwood lookin' ass nigga was offering me a job.

He said, "That's a measly ten grand in there, but it gets better. I'll give you ten per week for security purposes. You'll also get to venture off into some of the other shit you love." He held his gaze. "For me, though." He looked me in my eyes.

"The payments for any extra assignments will double and add to whatever our agreement is at the time as a bonus. What do you say?" He dumped his ashes.

Vulnerable, I wasn't where I wanted to be financially. I felt like I was starving! I took that job eleven years ago today. From that day forth, I rode with him to bust moves. I robbed, stabbed, shot, tortured, and suffocated niggaz at his command. I'd saved his life on numerous occasions, but, no more. Somebody did him dirty. I'm still confused on how he was touched. He never left the house alone. Congo and Spree said they'd left him and Teem out at the mansion after they'd went out.

My dude, he'd made me a wealthy man as to where I'll never have to struggle again. Now he's gone and his young ass nephew Zoo got the keys to the streets. He's already puttin' his lil niggaz in position to take over. Cuppy just flew in from Jamaica, and Fatima done disappeared with the bag. I'd stopped by her house this morning. Her car was out there, but I ain't get no answer. Hussle and Congo out there trying to track her down so we can try to figure out what happened. If she's dead, they ain't mentioned it.

Now here it is, I can't attend my nigga's funeral because I'm hot. I know them people gon' be out there taking flicks of the squad. No doubt, they'll definitely be on the lookout for a response to his murder. What me and Ross gon' do is get up outta here for a second. I need to go see my momma anyway. But first we got a few things that need to be taken care of.

# Chapter 7

## *LIL' ZOO*
## *Heir To the Throne*

It was 12:42 a.m. just days after J.L.'s demise so the block was still mourning. While a handful of my niggaz knew what went down, the rest of the hood was still trying to figure out the grizzly puzzle set before them. Me and my most trusted were at the spot on 32nd getting fucked up. We'd held a session there earlier that afternoon. Everybody showed besides Ross and Po. They were missing in action. Me, Proof, Brando, True, Fatal, Who-Man, Wales and Mighty were all in rotation on the Mary Jane.

"Zoo, my nigga, shit's crazy out here," U-Tee's voice dragged as he slouched in the armchair. He didn't smoke but he'd downed a pint of Remy and was working on another.

"Hell yeah," I replied, taking a pull of the green, then passing it to Wales. "I know everybody got word about the meeting. I wonder why them niggaz ain't show?" I sighed.

U-Tee said, "Them fools gotta be with Cup. I heard she just flew in."

"Damn." I shook my head. "You probably, right. I know she gotta be hurting, right now."

Brando corrected me, "Hurt ain't even the word, dog. Let me hit that shit. That lady devastated. No doubt." After hitting the weed a few times, he blew out the smoke and said, "Whew! Can you imagine the bullshit she's about to be on with niggaz?"

True said, "She gon' demand some answers. That's for damn sure. But fuck all that! You the king now, nigga! We supposed to be celebrating."

I snapped. "King? At what price? My muthafuckin—"

"Come on, Zoo," U-Tee interjected. "You know he didn't mean to—"

"I need to make shit clear so it's never misunderstood! At what cost, my nigga? My momma? The niggaz we buried? I didn't ask for none of this shit!"

Mighty butted in, "That ain't the point. The nigga Jay always said you were next up. Now you callin' it for us. You got it. The youngest nigga to ever run Burleigh. So, hold yo' crown."

"What?" I looked at him, wearing a mug.

"Our niggaz. Yo' momma. We gon' ride down for 'em or what?" Who-Man asked.

"You know that!" I replied. "What the fuck you think?"

"Enough said." Who-Man sank back into the couch.

Wales leaned forward on the sofa. "Now we talkin'. We out of greenery, though, niggaz. I'm about to go holla at Tallie and grab some more. Proof you riding?"

Proof stood up and stretched. "Yeah, I'll roll with you. That nigga owes me fifty, I need mine." He pulled a Glock 17 from his waist and cocked it. "You gon' let me dip, right?"

Wales said, "I was, but if you gon' kill 'em over that petty ass change you need to stay here."

"Did I say I was gon' murk him?" Proof frowned, stuffing his gun back in his pants. "You be trippin'. Worrying about the wrong shit. And why is it always petty when a muthafucka owe the next nigga his? Anybody need anything from the store while we out?"

"Grab me a big bag of CHEETOS and a 2-liter of Dr. Pepper. You can keep the change, lil' nigga," said Fatal.

"I was gon' keep it anyway." Proof smiled.

"Whatever, my nigga." Fatal laughed him off.

"Anybody else?" Proof asked.

"Nah," replied the others.

"A'ight, when we get back don't ask for none of my shit! We out." Wales was already heading out the door.

Who-Man yelled, "Tell that nigga Wales to grab some more Zags and a couple 40s!"

"A'ight," Proof replied.

He threw his hoodie up over his head and slid out of the crib into the morning's brisk air.

# Chapter 8

## *ZOO*
### *Applying Pressure*

As Proof stepped outside, he saw his cousin had already made it to the candy coated Eighty-eight on 30s and Royal Seals. His big cuz Wales had him by a few years. Wales had his own shit. A car, a crib and a mother and a father that loved him. Plus, he kept a bad bitch. Proof actually looked up to him, though he'd never tell him. Coming from an abusive family, Proof's father is someone he'd never met.

He often studied the faces of older men he'd run across in search of features he saw when he looked in the mirror. He often wondered if random strangers could possibly be his father? His mother had beat him more times than he'd like to remember when they lived in Chicago. Her addiction to cocaine turned her into a distant shadow of her former self. This in which drove him to the streets. His mother was clean now. The move to Milwaukee had been a blessing for them both. His father was from Wisconsin, so it gave him hope that he'd somehow find him.

Cuz said he'd help. Wales was always trying to look out for him. But Proof and his best friend Mighty stayed in some shit. Three years apart in age, the two were like Batman and Robin. Wales didn't like Mighty at all. He felt Mighty was a snake that fed off other nigga's pain. He hated that Mighty had followed his cousin from Chicago. He also secretly envied how Burleigh niggas had welcomed him in.

Before Proof arrived, Burleigh Zoo's young were known Disciples. They'd embraced Proof and Mighty in as Brothers. Mighty being the older of the two, Wales simply thought he'd know better. Though Proof was far from being an angel, Wales felt Mighty was a bad influence in his cousin's life. Mighty had it set in his mind that his gun would solve any and every problem or obstacle they'd run across. It's more than likely the reason Zoo welcomed him into the family. Wales wanted to show Proof something different. He kept him away from his crazy ass friend as much as he could. Wales decided to teach Proof, who'd just turned sixteen how to drive.

***

Outside the spot, looking first to the left, then ticking his head to the right Proof checked his surroundings. It was a habit. Trusting his instincts had kept him alive on many occasions. All was quiet on the block. Walking to the curb, he looped around the hood of the car and got in the driver's seat. Wales handed him the keys. Putting the key in the ignition, Proof turned it and the engine roared to life. Adjusting the seat and the rearview mirror, he slowly pulled off.

"Yo' lil' ass hit something I'ma fuck you up," Wales warned him.

"Aw, shut up, fool. I ain't gon' hit nothing. What you waiting on? Turn some music on in this bitch!"

"Hell nall, I don't want you bobbing ya head to a god-damn thing. Just stay focused on the road, nigga."

"Maaan!" Proof grinned crookedly.

"Little ass boy!" Wales laughed. "You lucky I'm letting you drive period. You ain't never drove this late. It's way past your curfew. You ain't supposed to be out here."

"You right. Fuck it. Who-Man said grab some more Zags and some beer."

"He send some money?"

"Nah, but Fatal did. He wants a big bag of Cheetos and a 2- liter of Dr. Pepper."

Proof went for his pocket. "Grab me a chocolate milk, two Suzi Q's and some Doritos."

He swerved and almost hit an oncoming car trying to get the money out of his jeans.

Wales panicked, grabbing the wheel.

"Whoa! Whoa! Brake-brake! Hit the brakes, nigga! Pull this muthafucka over!"

"Chill, nigga! I got it! Damn. I was trying to get the money."

"Don't worry about it! I got it, just pull over."

"Look. We here now." They were pulling into the Amaco on Burleigh and Sherman where Tallie posted 24-7.

"Pull up at the pump and slide over when I get out. I'm driving back."

"A'ight," Proof said. "There go Tallie, right there. Tell that nigga this me with you and run that fifty in cash or bud."

Wales pulled out a knot. He flipped through it and slid a fifty off.

"Here." He handed it to Proof. "We getting that in weed. I need some for the crib anyway."

"My nigga, don't be playin'. Grab the weed. Get whatever you gon' get from the window and let's go."

As always, Tallie stood in the station's lot next to the commercial Dumpster.

"Just get cha ass in the passenger seat," Wales sneered playfully with raised eyebrows.

He opened the door and got out.

"Don't forget my shit, cuz!" Proof yelled just before the door slammed.

Pocketing the fifty, he pulled his Glock and slid in the passenger seat as the interior lights faded. This particular gas station was known for robberies that didn't end well. Multiple murders had occurred at this location. The bullet proof glass and the white constructed brick foundation were riddled with bullets that never penetrated the Arab's bunkered walls. He served his customers through a sliding drawer after 9:00 P.M.

Proof laid his seat all the way back, keeping his eyes peeled for anything suspicious. Another car pulling in the gas station caught his attention. It was a car full of women. They didn't see him being that he was laying behind tint. One thing was for sure. Light skinned niggaz were in style back then, and Wales was a known ladies man. The true definition of a cock hound. Cursing himself for coming, Proof knew this nigga running into some hoes would keep them there longer than they needed to be. Proof didn't recognize the females. But clearly, they knew Wales.

"Wales! What's up, baby!" Two of the four ladies in the vehicle were hanging out of the windows of the navy-blue Jeep Cherokee.

"Shit! Y'all," Wales replied, finishing his transaction with Tallie.

He walked toward the truck wearing a smile as Tallie fell back under the cover of darkness.

*This nigga ain't even get the food,* Proof thought.

He was thinking about pussy. Nothing more, and nothing less. Just as Wales approached the females, two niggaz wearing all black emerged from the other side of the building carrying assault rifles.

One of the female occupants screamed, "Uh-uh! Bitch, look!"

Wales turned, and they sped off. Proof opened his door and rolled out dumping as they raised their weapons.

*Tat! Tat! Tat! Tat! Tat! Tat! Tat! Tat! Tat! Tat!*

They hit the homie up.

*Bak! Bak! Bak! Bak! Bak! Bak!*

"Waaaales!" He bucked blindly as he ran for cover, knowing if he'd stopped, he was as good as dead.

Tallie vanished over the fence behind the gas station, Proof followed his lead. He threw himself over the fence as well and the gun slipped from his hand, smacking the concrete on the other side. He hit the ground hard, landing on his back. The pain kept him conscious. He drew a deep breath. His will to live allowed him to scurry to his feet. Grabbing the Glock, he'd taken off just as another set of rounds sprayed the fence sending slugs whizzing past him.

Though Tallie was known to stay armed, he was nowhere in sight. Proof was running as fast as his legs would take him. The halogen lamps above burning in his mind like butane torches as his head and back throbbed from his fall. It seemed as though all the houses on the block were abandoned. Though porch lights gleamed, there was no signs of life. To most hearing shots were nothing unusual in the decaying urban community.

Aware of his surroundings, he headed toward Red Snapper and the corner store that stood across the street from it. Suddenly a car came screeching around the corner in front of him. The blaze of its headlights lit up the block as the high beams flashed. His gut instinct pushed him behind one of the trees that lined the block. The car crawled past him. The passenger was masked and leaning out of the window with an AK-47. His Glock was no match for the choppers they possessed.

"You see his lil ass?" He heard one of them ask.

He pressed his body against the bark of the maple tree hoping he blended in like a chameleon. He was out of breath, praying that he wasn't spotted.

As the dark Sedan crept up the block, he peeked out from behind the tree. When the taillights brightened and the white lights kicked in indicating that they were reversing, he darted across the street. He began squeezing off a few more rounds from the .17 as he did so.

*Bak! Bak! Bak! Bak! Bak! Bak!*

He'd managed to shatter the back window, but they were still on his ass. The chase was on again.

Dipping through a yard across the street, his mind raced in thought. Hearing the tires squealing and the thunder of the chopper had his soul shaken. He'd made it to the alley. Looking for a place to hide, he was running out of options. He chose to dive in a garbage can. There was silence for what seemed like an eternity, until he heard the cars cylinders pumping as they crept through the alley.

Seconds later, he heard a sound he'd often dreaded. But now the tocsin was like music to his ears. He heard sirens wailing that seemed to be close by. He wasn't safe just yet, so he stayed put. The sirens could easily mean the Arab had called about Wales laying out there in his lot and an ambulance was underway. Then, at times the sound of Police didn't mean shit to niggaz with this type of weaponry.

He could sense their presence. They couldn't have been more than a few feet from the garbage can he was in. He heard broken glass and gravel being crushed beneath the car's tires. The brake pads screaming as the driver eased up on the pedal, then applied pressure again and again. Then, finally relief.

"Fuck that nigga. We gotta bail! Come on, nigga, get in!" He heard a voice that sounded strangely familiar for some reason.

*Who the fuck is that?* he thought.

Hearing a car door slam, the motor rose and they sped off. Proof stayed in the can for hours. He was twisted by, yet another blow life had thrown. By the time, the coast was clear of police and he'd climbed out, the sun was up. He had a long walk back to the hood, and an even crazier story to tell on how they'd just lost his cousin Wales.

# Chapter 9

## *LI'L ZOO*
**Close**

I was hungover and still fucked up from the night before. Who-Man, Fatal, Mighty, True and the hoes we had come through didn't leave till six something that morning. It felt like I'd just closed my eyes. Then at about 7:05 a.m. I pried my lids open, to someone banging on the door like the police. *Who the fuck?* I'm pretty sure me in the big homey were thinking the same thing.

We were both clutching when U-Tee got up and opened the door. Proof fell in that bitch in tears.

"Fuck, my niggas! Y'all ain't heard? They shot him! They shot him, dog. They got cuz!"

"Who? Slow down!"

"They who? Who got shot? Tee asked.

"Wales!"

I raised off the couch. "Where the nigga at? Is he a'ight?"

He shook his head. "Nall, he dead."

"Where was y'all at?" Tee asked, as Proof pulled his gun from his waist and flopped down in the chair.

He ejected the slide. It was empty. "We were at a gas station on Burleigh and Sherman! He was talking to some females in a truck. Two niggas wearing masks came from the other side of the building and ate him up." He hung his head, then said, "I rolled outta the car. I'm backpedaling, bussin'! I ran, barely making it out of there. I hit the fence. They chased me but—"

"Who did it?" I asked.

"I don't know! Fuck, I swear I recognized one of their voices. It's like they knew me or something, but I can't—" He pounded his forehead.

U-Tee said, "Chill, young dog. Once you get your mind right, it'll come to you. What took you so long to get back? And what the fuck is that smell?" Tee frowned.

He looked at Tee. "Whoever fool 'nem was, they wasn't playin'! They was sprayin' shit! Look—" He stood up. "You see all this shit all over my clothes?" Spreading his arms, he said, "They hit cars, houses, trees and some more shit! See all these different colors y'all seeing? It's probably fiberglass, paint chips, somebody's windshield and sawdust how they was bussin at my ass. So, I climbed in a garbage can!"

I said, "Damn!"

He replied, "Yeah, no bullshit. Add that to the mix. The police being everywhere more than likely saved my ass. I swear to God they was right there. Then sirens. I told cuz! I told'em, get that shit and just... Damn!" he threw the Glock across the living room.

"Tallie? Was he out there?" Tee questioned.

"Yeah, but he hit it, too."

"What happened to the hoes?" I asked.

He said, "They pulled off as soon as they saw them niggas come around that building with that heat." He shook his head.

"He have any beef you know of?" I asked.

"Hell nall. You know blood ain't do shit but get money and fuck on a few bitches. If one got a problem, we all do. I can't believe I watched him get murdered right in front of me."

As he said that, Brando walked back in coming from the store. He said, "Dog, I just saw Wales car at the gas station over there off Burleigh and Sherman! They got shit all taped off. What the fuck happened?"

# Chapter 10

## *GINA*

At the funeral, I didn't know what to do. Witnessing her pain made me weak. Standing next to the casket, head hung, face streaked—she looked tired. It had been a long while since we'd been this close together. Feeling my presence, her eyes met mine. I nodded, and she surprisingly did the same. Drawing a deep breath, I thought for a minute trying to find the right words, but nothing came out. The way she looked at me and my baby, I just wanted to grab her and hold her. Her expression of acceptance suddenly changed. Her grief turned cold as she noticed Fatima standing behind me. Her eyes mixed with malice and curiosity, she gave me this long searching look.

This is what bothers me most, not knowing what she's thinking. I couldn't tell whether she'd shook her head in disgust or disbelief, probably both. After days of whining and all her begging, Fatima had finally persuaded me into being her escort this morning. Seeing me with someone who is more than likely to be her nemesis, there was no doubt she was feeling like I'd betrayed her once again. I just wanted to make sure nothing happened to this girl on my watch. She should've known by now that protecting people was part of my job description. We were simply there to pay our respects. We didn't stay. The church was packed with known dealers and killers. I knew my arrival caused a lot of discomfort.

This was their world! Most of these heathens knew I was a cop. In their minds, I was invading their territory. They had not a clue as to my relation to the deceased wife. Neither did Ms. Cage.

We got outta there, I dropped my daughter Angie off at school, and now we were on our way to the airport.

"Listen, Fatima, I'ma need you to disappear like a ghost. Don't come back here until I tell you it's safe. You understand?"

"Yeah, but—"

"But my—ass! You wanna live don't you? I gotta chase shit down. We've got clues, but we don't have a solid suspect yet!"

"Have you questioned Avarice? You see the way she was just starin' at me? I told you!"

"Yeah, she's been questioned, but I couldn't do it. It's a long story."

Giving me this long stare, she said, "Wh—why? Why couldn't you?"

"Just couldn't do it," I said! "Hell, don't be questionin' me! This is an ongoing investigation! I can't divulge that kind information. You just getcha ass on this plane and take yo' ass to Baltimore, D.C., New York or wherever you're headin! You said you headin' East, right?"

"Yeah, I'ma go see my momma. I thought I mentioned she lives in Bos—"

"I know-I know! But shouldn't nobody else know. You got my card. You didn't tell nobody where you're headin', right?"

"Just Lex," she replied.

"You told who! Oh, my God! You gon' get yourself killed. Didn't I tell yo' ass not to open yo' damn mouth? I don't know what I'ma do with you! Did you call her from my house! You know I did a background check on ya lil' friend with her theivin' ass!"

"I—I'm sorry. I was just—" She lowered her head as tears welled up in her eyes.

She'd almost made me curse myself, but I didn't. I stayed calm, for both of our sakes. "Girl, you got a lot of nerve. Don't start all that cryin'!"

I was trying to keep her alive. I'd been looking out for her all of two weeks. I'd invited her into my home. I fed her the best I could. Being that she was grief stricken, I had to coax her into eating period. J.L. had done it again. He'd taken another young girl that was too young to know any better and turned her out. As we rode in silence my mind was still at the church. I could've kicked his damn casket over just thinking of all the pain he'd caused. Hopefully, time would mend their hearts and nobody else would be hurt by his past actions. When we got to the airport, I waited with Fatima until she was ready to board her flight. Though we hadn't known each other long, she gave me a hug.

"Thank you!" she cried. "I hope I wasn't too much trouble?"

"None at all. Yo' ass just hardheaded." I smiled. "You actually remind me of somebody."

"Who? I know you ain't talkin' about Angie. She's so sweet and she's nothing like me."

"She bet—not be!" I laughed.

She said, "Damn, am I that bad?"

"Fatima, I did my homework on you as well. You've got a past but let it be just that. You got enough to start over now."

"But who is it that I remind you of?" she questioned.

I said, "My sister. Believe it or not, you two were just alike. The way I see it, you're the lucky one. Now get outta here. Call me when you land."

"Will do—again, thank you Ms. Gina."

"You're welcome. Gon' now. And don't forget what I told you!"

She looked back and smiled, as I waved goodbye.

# Chapter 11

## *MOO*

The sun was low in the sky as we rode behind tint in the green conversion van we'd dubbed *The Hulk.* I'd decided to let Davin ride shotgun so we could chop it up, He'd become antsy. In my mind, I imagine he and his brother were as desperate for revenge as me and mine. Doe and the young boy's older brother were in the back with two street sweepers as we slid through traffic.

"Man, we been lookin' for these niggaz for a month!" Davin frowned impatiently.

I corrected him, "Nah, lil' dog. Y'all only been up here for two weeks—"

"Shit, it feels like a month," he replied.

"Chill. We can't find the niggaz. Maybe, we'll have to improvise." I hit the weed and inhaled. "I might kick it with you tonight." I blew my smoke out. "Show you how to get some money the ski mask way. You say you been layin' niggaz down?" I passed him the joint.

"I been coppin' bricks and wreckin' shit for years!" Davin boasted before taking a toke and holding in the smoke. "Niggaz better ask about me."

"Lil nigga, you what—five-two? How you gon' rob somebody?" Doe said, still peering out the back window.

He exhaled. "That's what makes it so easy. Mufuckaz never expect it. They don't see it until I'm right up on 'em."

"What if a nigga grabs you?"

"Ain't no nigga grabbin' shit!"

I could tell this was something he hadn't given much thought to before he answered. He probably thought it was something that couldn't happen because it *hadn't* happened. Young boy had a lot to learn. So, I decided to school 'em. Give 'em one of the deadly tricks of the trade.

"Listen, my nigga. Beauty is always here." I grabbed the .44 that rested in in my lap as I drove. I held it up, then set it back down.

"But the beast lies here." I tapped the chest plate of the vest beneath my shirt.

"So, what chu sayin'?" he questioned.

"Never underestimate the heart of a man. I've seen niggaz go for the gun, I mean go straight at a nigga and take the banger. Predator becomes prey. When's the last time you shot somebody, cuz?"

"When!" He laughed. "Bruh, you hear this nigga up here? Fuck kind of question is that? We see these niggaz! I'ma—"

"Nah, that ain't what I'm sayin'. Calm down. Check me out. What I'm askin' is, did a nigga make you shoot 'em? Or, was you gon' pop'em anyway? There's a difference. You gotta take control. When I strip a nigga, I get on his ass literally. I get up behind him and put that iron to his ass. Right to the crack of that mufucka. Pops gave me the game early on. Before a nigga moves anything else, he gotta move his ass. If a bitch flinch wrong—I got two for 'em. The first one is for movin' when I told his ass not to. The second one is just a reflex."

The niggaz started laughin'. "Hey, I'm serious. Make sure the thought of disarming you never crosses a mufucka mind. You hear me? I know y'all niggaz hungry, cause I am," I said, pulling into the burger joint on Capitol and Fondulac.

Eric said, "Hell yeah! You read my mind."

Doe said, "Hold on, Moo! Ain't that—ain't that the bitch Kia car pullin' in that parking spot over there?"

Eric said, "That look like the car that was in front of that crib we was layin' on a few days ago!" I looked, and sure as shit stank it was her. She got out of the Cutty, thicker than all out-doors!

Davin said, "Damn! Who is that!"

I said, "Po baby momma."

"I got her. Let me get this bitch." Davin reached for the door handle about to get out.

"Nigga, yo' lil' ass barely got hair on your face! That bitch ain't gon—"

"Watch this." Davin smiled and jumped out of the van.

Unaware of the ill—fated danger, Lil' Davin was standing right behind her in ZaZa's as she placed her order.

"Let me get six gyros. Some fries—" Kia scanned the menu.

"How many orders?" the female behind the counter asked.

"Uh, six," she replied, taking her time.

"That'll be twenty-one-forty-seven." the lady turned to call the order.

"Did I say I was done!" Rekia rolled her eyes.

"That's not all?" She turned back and asked with sheer attitude.

"Nah, bitch! How you gon' rush me?" Rekia huffed.

"Mm—mm—mmm! Damn, girl, don't be so mean. You sharin' all that?" Davin uttered just loud enough for her to hear.

She looked back and smiled, as he undressed her with his eyes.

"Nah, boy, this for me, my kids and a few friends." She rolled her neck, checkin' him out.

"I ain't talkin' food. I'm talkin' about all that ass." He smiled.

She said, "Lil boy, please. You wouldn't know what to do with all this pussy if I gave it to you. So, stop," she continued to glance at the menu.

"Gimme that mufucka and see then," he replied.

She sucked her teeth. "You just a baby."

"*A baby?* I'm grown. My pockets grown too! What's up?" He pulled two wads out of his hoodie that he could hardly palm.

"Boy! Who you think you talkin' to! I ain't no hoe!" She grinned, tossing that ass from left to the right as she shifted her weight.

"Um, excuse me! Are you gonna order or not!" The woman behind the register grew agitated.

"That's probably yo' momma rent money." She turned back toward the counter.

"Damn bitch. My bad. Let me get six milk shakes, two double cheeseburgers with bacon and two orders of onion rings. Oh, and two Pepsis!" She yelled, being that the lady taking the order had stepped away from the counter. She turned to Davin. "I tell you what—if that money's yours like you say it is, you can pay for this food for me. I may return the favor by giving you something to eat." She smiled.

He shook his head. "Hell nall—rent money. Remember?"

She smacked her lips. "Em-hmm! I knew yo' lil' ass was frontin'."

"Nah, how much is that shit? You gon' give a nigga somethin' to eat, huh. Mrs—"

"Rekia, if you can fit it all in your lil' mouth."

"Talk nasty to me then."

"That'll be thirty-six-seventy-seven." He peeled off a hundred-dollar bill, handing it to the cashier. "Keep the change."

Rekia said, "Let me stop. What's your name anyway? I ain't never seen you around here before."

"They call me, Kaboo," he lied. "I ain't from around here."

"Well, Kaboo, I'ma give you my number." She went in her purse and got an ink pen. "Give me your hand. I ain't got no paper." She wrote her number on his palm. "Call me, I'ma make breakfast in the morning. You can come through and get a plate."

"A plate? I know you got a nigga. I come through I'm tryin' to get more than a plate."

She said, "Don't worry about my nigga. That's not a problem. If he was going to be there, you wouldn't be comin' to get shit. Just make sure you fill those pockets up—you plan on gettin' anything extra." She smiled, grabbed her food, and headed out.

"What time should I call?" he asked.

"Around seven. My kids will still be sleep." Her hands were full as she opened the door with her butt and dipped out.

He soon followed, she was just about to get in her car, when he called out to her.

"Say, Rekia, hold up for a second!"

"What's up!" She watched, as he jogged over to her.

She was shocked when he upped the 2nd Generation .45 and pressed it against her stomach.

"Bitch, if you scream or make any sudden moves, I'ma kill yo' ass right here. Come on. We goin' to this van over here."

# Chapter 12

## *HOOD*
## *Fuckin' Wit' the Wrong Nigga*

Tipp had taken a trip, she felt was very much needed. Her and her sister on her father's side were vacationing in Florida. They were calling it a retreat. It was late, I was tired from basketball practice. Walking in the crib after school, I went to my room, dropped my book bag, I took off my coat. I kind of thought my mind was playin' tricks on me when I heard what sounded to me like a woman's cry followed by laughter. I then heard Moo and Doe's voices coming from downstairs in the basement.

I also heard voices I didn't recognize. Scratches was down there barking, goin' crazy! She was only about eleven months but, she'd developed a helluva attitude. Growlin' and tryin' to bite people and shit!

*Mula gone have to come get this crazy—ass dog! And today!* I thought as I went downstairs to see what was goin' on.

I was thinking the twins' nasty asses was probably down there fuckin' some lame chick that was weak for dollars. It wouldn't be the first time I'd interrupted their fun train.

*Habba! Habba! Habba! Habba! Habba!* Scratches yapped angrily.

Bloody foam oozing from her mouth as she stood on her back legs. Launching forward, she attempted to break free of Moo's grasp on her silver linked collar.

*Habba! Habba!* She barked, then made these sharp peremptory sounds. It was as if she was actually trying to speak.

"Watch! Watch her mama! Watchhh! Watch that bitch!" Moo spoke in this weird uncanny high-pitched voice as if he were talking to a baby. Like he understood her yawping.

Two other niggaz I didn't know stood by laughing as the dog strived to get free. They were both real short. One looked like *Childish Gambino*. He wasn't even wearing a fuckin' shirt. Just jeans, and a bulletproof vest. He had half of his nappy afro braided. I mean, just country. He took a swig of the fifth of Henny he held by the neck of the bottle.

The other was well dressed from head-to-toe, but too young for the particular scene before me. In a Celtics snap—back and hoodie to match, he wore this wicked grin. Lookin' like a much younger and skinnier version of Ja Rule.

"Let me hit that yak, bruh!" He reached for the Cognac.

They hadn't even heard me come down over all the noise Scratches was making.

"What the hell!" I'd gained their attention wearing a look of confusion.

Moo mugged, as he hushed me. I glanced at Doe, but he averted my gaze. They all quickly directed their attention back toward the female cuffed to the support beam in the center of the basement. Her clothes were thrown about, she was naked, blindfolded and gagged. There were a pair of black panties stuffed in her mouth, that I reckoned were her own.

Scratches had gnawled her legs and her feet as she laid helplessly on her back on the cold basement floor. She struggled, and soon managed to push the panties from her throat using her tongue. She looked exhausted as she let out another cry.

"He—help meee," she moaned.

That's when the light bulb flashed in my head. I recognized her!

"Damn, that's—that's Kia!" I whispered.

"Hit that bitch!" Moo commanded.

Letting Scratches go, her paws scraped against the pavement as she scurried in sliding on the attack. Grabbing one of Kia's breasts, she shook it ferociously. Feeling her pain, I fucked around and clutched my chest.

"Oh—oh shit! She got her titty! She got her titty! Ha—haaa!" Gambino yelled, jumping up and down in excitement.

Moo said, "Bitch you gon' talk, huh? You wanna talk now!"

She screamed, "Aaahhh! Aaaahhhh! Okkaayyy! Okkaayyy! Make it stop! Get it off meee! Get it off! The-they in Chi-Chicago! They in Chi-Chicagooo! Aaaahhh!"

"Moo laughed. "I told y'all asses she'd hit somethin'!

"Tu-tu-tu! Scratches, let her go! Let her go and bring yo' ass here!" he called her off.

She ran to him, but the damage had already been done. They'd let the dog bite her up, taking mouthfuls from her thighs. The shit had me feeling a little squeamish, so I ran back upstairs trying to hide the revolt and threatening nausea. There was a knock at my door a few minutes later as I laid across my bed. It was Doe. He gave me some insight in hope that I'd understand.

He reminded me that the nigga that had tried to kill him and Jah was still out there. I couldn't help but think about Teague and his saying, *"The streets will never close."* It rings true. Though, he was home, and J.L. was quite dead, the drama was far from being over. The two niggaz in the basement with Moo were Janahdah's brothers. They were back in the Mil on a mission. They'd searched high and low for the niggaz Po and Ross, but they were nowhere to be found.

I guess they were counting on them being hellbent on revenge following the demise of their leader. Since his death hadn't brought them out, they had to come up with other means of conflict with the expectation of a forced showing of hands. This in which led them to Ms. Rekia Thompson. One might say, she was just in the wrong place at the wrong time. Po's baby momma probably ain't have nothin' to do with nothin' up or down. Blindly, her man's doings had set her on a crash course of destruction. Fuckin' with the wrong nigga.

***

When Cyn finally got here, we were done eating. I was loading the dishwasher. We heard her horn beep twice as she set her alarm.

"Lue, go get the door. That's Cyn."

"Hood, I'm full. I can't move!"

"Girl! Getcha ass up and go open the damn door. Ain't nobody tell yo' ass to eat all them pancakes." I smiled.

"A'ight, dang." She moped out of the kitchen.

"Hood, she dead?" Bri asked.

"Pit Bull Rekia?" I chuckled. "Em-mm. They let her live, in order to send a message. As crazy as it may sound, the twins called it gettin' up with her glamour. That girl's face is marred, she got one titty, seven toes and some bit up thighs. She died some."

"Hey, y'all! What's up? What y'all talkin' about? Who died? Where's the food? I smell it."

"We ain't talkin' about nothin'just how a bitch got herself fucked up, fuckin' with the wrong nigga. Ring any bells?" I smiled.

Ignoring me, she went straight for her breakfast. Pressing the button on the microwave, she opened it, looked at her plate, closed it back and set the timer.

She said, "Hood, I ain't got time for your jokes this morning. You funny, but I'm hungry. I take it that's a no as far as goin' to Racine's tonight?"

"What's wrong with them niggaz comin' up here? We had fun the last time we were all together."

"I agree. We did, huh?" Cyn replied.

Mula said, "Mufuckaz do a lil too much bangin' up that way for me. I know we bang out for money, but them niggaz is just too stupid.

"I said, "Cyn, I don't like that nigga. You can do better."

"You just said we had fun the last time we were all together. Why you hate him so much?" Cyn asked.

"Because he ain't shit!" I frowned. "His ass better be glad I love my niece and my nephews. Racine—ass nigga."

"Aw, shut up, Hood. What about me? You don't love me? And what chu know about a Racine nigga?" she asked, grabbing her plate.

"Bitch, you know I luh you. Eat!" I waved her off.

# Chapter 13

## *PO*

We shot back up here from the Chi as soon as we heard about what happened with my girl. She's been in the ICU fucked up ever since we got here. It's been three days now. They say she lost a lot of blood and had to undergo emergency surgery. The doctors tell us they're pretty confident she's going to make it. However, they told Rekia's mother that she miscarried due to the attack, believed to be by a dog.

According to the family, the police are unsure if it was more than one. She'd been carrying for eight weeks. All this is a shock to me, because she hadn't mentioned anything about being pregnant. She was found naked in front of the firehouse on 30th and Galena. The hood has been going crazy trying to figure out what happened.

On the other hand, Cuppy is back. Although I've yet to see her, I know she wants blood behind J.L.'s murder. She's got a board meeting scheduled for tomorrow morning. She'd let it be known that she wanted every major figure that ate off her husbands' plate front and center. Her message to the streets was firm. Any nigga that don't show up, knows what time it is.

Since I've yet to find his killer, showing my face is the least I can do for my nigga. I have to roll through there, then get back here. When Kia woke up, I needed to holla at her and find out what the fuck went on. Everybody got their own theory. I know for damn sure she hadn't suddenly ran across a pack of wild hyenas that had torn all of her clothes off, and damn near killing her in the process.

Her friends told me she'd went to go pick up some food. That much makes sense. The Cutty was found in ZaZa's parking lot where I assumed she left it. So far, everybody we talked to claim they ain't hear or see nothing. It's getting late, and though I don't wanna leave the hospital, I gotta get up out of here. It's the only way I'll come up with some answers. Her sister got the shorties, so they're in good hands. In dealing with this shit, I can hardly cope.

Rekia's my baby, so I need something to ease the pain being that I can't soothe hers.

Strapped and ready, me and Ross jumped in his El Dog. I had him stop at Love's Liquor Store. I ran in and grabbed some bottles. Then we went and got at Tallie. I needed some smoke. Since she was found on G-Street, the first thing we did was slide back over on them N.W.A. niggas. Still, we got nothing.

I said, "Ross, ride down on Skinny."

"Come on, nigga!" he complained. "You know I—"

"Listen to me," I cut him off. "You'll be a'ight as long as you don't fall into his trap. Don't argue with him. Whatever, and I mean whatever his little ass say just agree with him." Ross looked at me and sighed.

He said, "A'ight."

"I'm tellin' you! If you fall for his bullshit, we'll be there from now until the sun come up. Just chill."

"I hear you." He shook his head and continued to drive.

Skinny was like an Almanac when it came to certain shit like sports, movies and guns, but sometimes he got it wrong. We're human. One time we almost crashed and came to blows, because I'd said I was a fan of Janet Jackson. I said, I love her and wouldn't hesitate in copping front row tickets to see her live concert. I guess he was raised differently. See, his father was a pimp.

So, my nigga has it in his mind that a woman is, and always will be beneath him. To him, they were unworthy, scandalous hoes. They were only good for fucking, sucking, selling pussy, washing his drawers, ironing and bringing their money to him. I'd tried my best to remind him that he too had a mother and a sister. A woman had also given birth to his seed. I asked, *"How can it be wrong for a man to love a woman such as Janet for what she does? Her beauty, personality on stage, sex appeal, music etcetera?"*

When he could turn around and say he'd buy a front row seat to see Scarface or any nigga for that matter. How can one claim to love a man out of relation to his music, but it's wrong to love a woman in that same fashion? How? It was like I was talking to a brick wall. He still didn't get it and I guess he thought he wanted to fight.

It was about to go down, when one of the homies stepped in and told him, "Think, over Janet?" Mind you, we're doing time and this nigga was slippin' literally. Fresh out of the shower, he ain't have on shit but some soggy drawers and some punk ass flipflops. He couldn't have weighed no more than a buck-twenty. A puppy, trying to rush a bull. He would've surely loss and was willing to. Simply because he hated being wrong. In his eyes, I was dead—wrong.

We got past it, though. It's now, something we can both - look back and laugh on. We'd pulled up on him. He was standing out on his front porch watching his child's mother work the block. Cold hearted, but I couldn't fault him. It had been a minute, so it's good to see 'em.

We shook up and embraced, then I ran the situation to him. He usually kept his ear to the jungle. To my surprise, he ain't have shit for me neither as far as who done it. Standing in the backyard of his spot, he hit the joint, exhaled and looked at me.

"Po, you're a real live scumbag."

I took no offense. This fool was the only nigga I'd ever known to use this particular term. To him, it meant a number of things. It all depended on his mood when he said it. It could be a compliment, or exactly what it is. A form of disrespect. Being a gangsta, doing dirty deeds means to survive. This means, gettin' it out the mud. So, I just looked at him and smiled, he stood there lookin' like a light-skinned Billy Ocean. He was rockin' a wave Nuvo, dressed in a white silk shirt, white slacks and some gators. My nigga swore he'd been pimpin' since pimpin' began.

"More than likely, the shit that happened because of yo' ass," he spoke with his hands.

"I know you got something on you. Le—let me see what you got." He held out his palm.

I pulled out the old trusty Dirty Harry long nose .44 and handed it to him. He grabbed it, looked at it, threw his head back and laughed.

Suddenly serious, he said, "That's garbage. Pu-put that little shit up. I ain't even gotta ask this other scumbag what he got," he said referring to Ross.

"What's that supposed to mean, nigga?" Ross said angrily.

"Exactly what I just said, nigga! You got the same two nines every time you come through this muthafucka," he spoke fast, in a comedic tone of Kevin Hart, but has more of a little man complex and swag like Kat Williams.

I looked at Ross, praying he didn't do it. Technically, Skinny was right. They might not have been the exact same pistols. But that same make and models, same guns.

He said, "Y'all ain't on shit!" He waved us off.

"Po, wipe my prints off that real quick."

He grabbed a duffel bag from under the porch. "You won't put no bodies on me," he mumbled, then turned back to us. "You wipe that off?"

I said, "Yeah, damn!"

"Don't yeah, me, nigga! Let me see you wipe off."

I said, "Come on, nigga. Stop playin'! What you got?" He held the bag to his frame.

"First, I wanna see you wipe-that-muthafucka down!" he said, stomping his feet to every syllable. I guess he thought it would make shit clearer.

He said, "You first, I ain't bullshittin'!"

"A'ight, check it. See?" I pulled the cannon out and rubbed the handle and the entire gun down with the front of my T-shirt.

"That's mo-better." He dropped the duffel bag and unzipped it.

He pulled out some sort of short rifle and handed it to me with a proud smile.

"What the fuck is that? A twenty-two?" Ross chuckled.

Skinny then reached inside the bag and fished out a handful of bullets. The rounds looked big enough to fit an AK-47.

He said, "That's a seven millimeter there, Playboy. Gone throw one of 'em in. That bitch is loud." I smiled and checked the pipe.

"Shit, you got the clip?" I asked.

He grabbed that as well.

"Yeah, it's right here." He handed it to me.

I loaded the clip, slid it in and cocked that joint. Pointing it towards the sky, I pulled the trigger. It was so loud, it woke Skinny's daddy out of his drunken slumber.

His Pops ran outside, chopper in his hand, screaming, "Wh—what was that! Wh-where my son! Where my son at!"

Laughing, Skinny called out to him from alongside of the house.

"Aye, I'm good Pops! It's all good. That was us. Gone back in the house."

His dad looked at him and said, "Boy! What the hell wrong with you? Whatever that is, y'all put that shit up! Don't shoot that damn thang no more. Woke me up out my damn sleep?" He saw us snickering. He said, "And what's so damn funny? The pimp is here!" He burped, and slowly strolled back in the crib.

We died laughing.

I said, "Dog, how much you want for this?"

"Listen. Ssss," Skinny hissed. "I fucks wit' you, so I'm gon' lookout for y'all. Gone take the bag. On my momma, it's a Mossberg pump in there, two Techs and a few more pistols. Way mo-better than that shit y'all got." He paused, then said, "Just do me this one favor." He hammered his fist into his palm.

"What's up?" I asked.

"When you find out who done this shit, put a few in 'em for me. Kia good, shit, I used to fuck with her cousin T-Kay. Now that fucked me up. I'd never heard this nigga express anything positive concerning women, at all. To hear him speak highly of mine told me he'd changed, if only a little.

Then he said, "Y'all get gone, though. This the hood, but they do popup on the East when they want to. Scumbags."

After another laugh, we thanked him, showed the pimp some love and hit it. I would definitely put the tools to use.

## Chapter 14

### *FATIMA*

'Tima, what you doing?" It was Lex.

I checked my watch, it was ten-fifteen at night here, but we're an hour ahead. Her ass was probably just gettin' off work.

"Nothing, bored. Sitting here in my fuzzy slippers and a house-coat."

"Damn! You're about to be what, twenty-four not nine. I know you ain't up there having no slumber party without me! Who's there?" She sucked her teeth.

"Girl, nall and my birthday ain't for another two weeks. It's just me, my mom, my aunties and a few of my cousins. They're in the other room, though. It's ladies night, bitch! We're goin' out to-night!"

"Bostonnn!" she yelled.

"Yee-ah, Lexi! See what these East Coast niggaz be like!" I re-plied, looking at my butt in the mirror.

She smacked her lips. "Girrlll, you bet not!"

"What? You know I ain't been out this way since I was six or seven or some shit. I'm just checkin' the scene. And why? You miss me?" I laughed.

She said, "Fatima, I don't see a damn thing funny!"

"I know, sorry, my bad."

"You ain't trying to dance, is you?"

"Bitch, no! My stripper days are done. You trippin'. Where my baby at?"

"Nomi? His lil' ass running around here. He swears he's a Ninja Turtle. He better sit his butt down somewhere before I beat him. Around here flippin' on all my shit."

"Hoe, you bet not touch my lil' man." We both laughed.

See, I don't usually fuck with bitches. They too damn shiesty, but me and Alexus go way back since elementary. She's my road dawg for real-for real. Back in the day, when me and my momma had just moved to the Hillside Apartments. I remember that shit just like it was yesterday. My daddy was long gone. To make matters worse, he'd left my mother for her so-called *best friend*. She was sick. That love, heartbroken sick. You know? She'd then turn to drugs. She'd lost so much weight back then, I thought she was gonna die. So, when I say we barely had a pot to piss in or a window to throw it out of—you can believe that shit.

*"Fatima, go next door and ask Mary if we can borrow some sugar," she told me the first night we'd gotten there.*

*I don't know how or what she thought she was gon' cook. In fact, she wouldn't, I would. I'd been grown since I was nine, I had to be. That Heroin had her leaning, rockin' and scratchin'. Yeah, the lady Mary smiled and introduced herself as her and her two kids watched us move our few boxes in, but that was it. She had a son that looked a few years my senior, but her daughter and I looked as if we could be around the same age. We'd shared a few glances at one another, as I wished my mother could braid my hair like she'd worn hers.*

*"Ma, we don't know them people!"*

*"What I just say lil' girl? Don't you sass me! Mind yo' mama! Goo! I'ma make some rice and fry us some chicken."*

*"Yes ma'am," I replied. "Shoot!" I stomped off, grumbling under my breath.*

*"Girl! Don't be stompin' or mumbling either! Keep it up, you hear!" she yelled. "What, you wanna eat salt? Hell."*

*"I didn't want to, but, I went and knocked on their door, Alexus answered.*

*"Hi," I said, just standing there, looking stupid.*

*"Hey," she replied, with a raised eyebrow.*

*"I think your hair is so—fly."*

*"Fly? What, I got a fly in my head?" She patted her head, getting grease all over her hands. "Is it gone?" She frowns, looks at her hands and wipes them against her pajamas.*

*"No, I didn't mean a bug was—"*

*"Girl, you talk funny." She smiled. "What does that mean then?"*

*"It means, dope, fresh. I like it. Who did it?" I asked.*

*"Okay. Fresh, that sounds better." She put her little hand on her hip. "My momma did it." she announced proudly. "I'm Alexus. What's your name?"*

*"Fatima," I said, shyly.*

*Then I heard her mother yell, "Lexus, who is that at my door!"*

*Her eyes got big. "Hold on." She held up one finger. "It's Fatima!"*

*"Fa—who!"*

*"Next door, ma!"*

*"Tell her, my—my motha wanna know—" I twiddled with my fingers nervously. "She said to ask your mom if we can borrow some sugar?"*

*"Oh, okay." she paused. "You wanna come in? My momma ain't gon' say nothin'."*

*"Yeah."*

*"Come on then."*

*I stepped inside, and she shut the door.*

*"Wait here, okay?"*

*I gave her a short nod. Looking around, their apartment was a replica of ours. But theirs had furniture and pictures on the walls.*

*"Maaaa!" She ran off into the small apartment and made a left toward her mother's room.*

*All I heard was, Fatima in the living room."*

*"What! Who? Some sugar? Yeah, tell your brother I said put them some in a cup."*

*A few seconds later, Lex's brother Red was handing me a white cup filled to the brim. Alexus was standing at his side. She smiled and said, "I'm gonna ask my mama if I can come play with you tomorrow after school, okay?"*

*"Okay. Thank y'all," I replied before I left.*

*That's how our friendship began. We'd started kickin' it damn near every day.*

*A few months in, I was coming back from the store when some chicks from another building tried me. They wanted my penny candy and the bag of donuts they'd just watched me buy. On some petty shit, they'd followed my ass, taunting me.*

*"Y'all hungry?" the one leading the pack asked.*

*"I want some doughnuts and she got some," I heard another say. They were about ten deep, and I was scared.*

*"She got candy, too!" said another.*

*I was steppin' as fast as I could.*

*Somebody said, "She's new to the hood. She don't know what's up. Look at her, trying to be all cute."*

*I was almost home. As I came up the hill, I could actually see Alexus and her cousin she'd told me was coming by that afternoon standing out front. So, I knew they saw me too. Then it was on.*

*One of the girls grabbed me from behind. "Come here! Give that shit up, bitch!" She tried to sling me, but I kept my balance.*

*I dropped the bag and started swinging. I was throwing my bands with all my might. They were on me, though. It was too many for me. I was thrown against a car, where I'd eventually balled up and just took the kicks and blows. A few seconds into the beating the odds changed. Lex and her cousin Queen had come to my rescue. All I know is the attack against me suddenly stopped.*

*I heard, "You hoes get up off her!"*

*I got up to see Lex and her cousin, who I'd never met standing back to back throwin' down on my behalf. We beat them bitches until they'd given up and ran off.*

*My little double dips and penny candy laid scattered from the sidewalk to the street. Crouched over holding my knees, I was completely out of breath, shirt torn, hair all over my head I looked over at Lex.*

*"Wh—what took y'all so long?" I asked. "They was beatin' my-my ass!"*

*Her big cousin laughed and said, "She wanted to help you right away. I wanted to see if you was gon' fight back. They had yo' ass!" She clutched my shoulder. "You fought back, though. I like that. You a young Sheek!"*

*I looked up at her and smiled. She was a couple years older than us. Light skinned, thick with real curly hair, Lex later told me her cousin was the leader of a crew called Sheek Girls. I wanted to be down.*

***

*"'Tima, you should just come home for your birthday. Your family got you now and forever. Y'all about to go kick it now. Just come spend your day with me. That's all I'm asking. You can fly right back."*

*"I don't know, Lex."*

*"Come on, girl!"*

*"Let me think about it. Have you heard anything on who killed Jay?"*

*"Nope, girl, I ain't heard shit about J.L. since he's been gone."*

*"Let me finish gettin' ready to go out. I'll call you back."*

*"Okay, girl. Have a drunk night." Lex laughed.*

*"Oh, I will. Love you."*

*"Love you, too."*

# PART 2

*The Book of Secrets*

# Chapter 15

## *HOOD*

My girl was glowing with excitement. I knew Cyn would be a devoted mother above all else, but the past few months were running through my mind like a movie in 3D, I couldn't do nothin' but shake my head. The night I introduced her to this fool. We'd barely made it out of the house. Now, I'm wishing we hadn't. Anyway, we were running late again. It was all my fault; I wasn't ready to leave just yet. We were about to go kick it with the niggaz again.

"Tramp will you come on!" Bri griped. "You called us like you was ready!"

I was in the bathroom mirror puttin' on my eyeliner. My new hairdo had me lookin' like a young Journey Smollett. "Bitch, I'm almost done! Getcha panties outta bunch. Them niggaz ain't goin' nowhere."

She said, "I ain't got on none! Now come on! You look good!"

"It's been twenty minutes, Hood." Sweets sighed.

"Chill, damn! Y'all buggin'. You know what? Get out! I don't know why all y'all in here anyway. I ain't call nobody in here but Lue!" They didn't budge.

Cyn said, "Nope, we ain't goin' nowhere." She crossed her arms, bobbling her head.

"Hood."

"Hmm? What's up, Lue?"

I paused with the pencil, popping then smeared my lips together evening out my cherry-red lipstick.

"When we gon' hit these niggaz pockets?"

Mula yelled, "Whoo! Check her out y'all! You sounding a lot like me young PYT! Let her know!" She gave Lue some dap.

"We ain't got time to just be out here cakin' with these niggaz! What they workin' with?"

I said, "Shit, I don't know. Y'all gotta ask Cyn."

Everybody looked at her to see if she had something to say.

"What?" She turned up her nose.

"You still down to touch 'em, right? Or, has that changed?" I questioned.

"I don't—I mean, yeah. Why not? They ain't gon' miss the money. But we ain't gon' kill nobody, right? We can hit 'em whenever y'all ready."

I said, "What do you mean we? You ain't going?"

"Bitch, I'm there," she snapped.

I wasn't stuntin' her ass.

Mula laughed. "Oohhh, let's get it! Sweets, I told you my palms were itching this morning, didn't I?"

Bri said, "Cyn, you know going in anything can happen? You sure?" Her hesitation told me she was having doubts.

"Yeah," she replied.

Glancing in the mirror once more, I said, "A'ight, I'm ready."

"About time," Bri hissed.

"Shut up!" I said. "You'll have more than enough time to show yo pretty little ass. Trust me."

They followed me to my room so I could grab my jacket. I'd just copped that red Michael Jackson leather with all the zippers. We were on our way out when we noticed Teague in the living room with Tipp. He was watching the game.

"Go—go—go-go!"

I murmured, "Hey, Teague!" I greeted him as we tried to mosey our way out the door. Bri already had it open.

He stopped us. "Hey-hey—hey!" we paused. "Where y'all goin? Come on in here!"

Bri closed the door, and we headed into the living room. I stomped in there like a five-year old.

"Aww mannn! Teague, come on now. We don't wanna watch no football." I knew we were in for one of his lectures. I flopped down on the couch.

My girls took seats beside me.

"Where y'all think y'all goin' this late?" he asked bitterly.

I'd seen this look far too many times by means of Moo and Doe.

"Uh, out. It's the weekend." Mula rolled her eyes.

He laughed, looking her up and down. Shaking his head, he said, "Out? Out where? Y'all ain't old enough to get in nothin' but trouble. It's past ya bedtime."

I said, "We goin' to the Vet, Teague."

"Red Corvette, huh?" He chuckled. "Dressed like that?"

"Dressed like what?" Cyn asked.

What she do that for?

"Like some two—dollar ho—"

Tipp attempted to add her two cents, but Teague cut her off.

"Hold on, sis, I got this. Now, y'all know it's a lot of ignorant niggaz out there that don't think and react off impulse."

Ain't nobody say shit, so naturally he zoomed in on me.

"Hood, you know that right?"

""Yeah, I know," I replied dryly.

"So, why y'all dress so damn provocative? You wanna get raped out there?"

"Teague, ain't no nigga—"

"Wait a minute now! Let me finish before you start poppin' that shit! I want y'all to hear me out on this. I tell no lies, nor claim easy victories. This world is cold. The penitentiary packed and the graveyard is full of men and women alike that doubted what a muthafucka would and wouldn't do. Sometimes, once you take it there ain't no coming back! Brianna—" He turned to her.

"What's up?" She looked nervous.

"Chess has been around, for what? About fourteen—hundred years?" He was challenging her mentally.

She said, "That's just over here. It actually dates back to AD six hundred in a piece of poetry from the Kashmir region."

"Umm-hm," he said. "You know your history. A wise man once said it's always been about those who've won. Tell me this. Why do you think the queen suddenly went from being the weakest, to the most powerful piece on the board?"

"Cause she's a bad bitch. Ooops!" She covered her mouth for a second. "Excuse my language, Ms. Tipp."

She smiled, half embarrassed, half pleased with her answer.

"Is that your final answer? Think' about it now."

She said, "Yup."

He said, "Close enough. It's because somebody, somewhere came to the realization that a woman is the most powerful being on this planet. This is true. Now, I ain't gon' tell y'all not to wear that shit, because I know you gon' do it anyway. I just want y'all to know your worth. Never forget, a woman's work is never done. Y'all are the foundation of our future. A man can't push out no babies."

I said, "So, what you saying, Teague?"

"What I'm saying is this, be careful. At times, what we love tends to destroy us. Protect yourselves. I just came from a process designed to break me. To separate me from my family. Black men are being hunted like animals, caged, and enslaved. If you pay attention, you'll see the trap. You all are the targets as well. Who do you think taking care of ninety—eight percent of niggaz locked up across Amerikkka?"

"A woman!" Mula blurted out with a smile.

"Ding! Absolutely. Without y'all we're nothing. Whitey recognizes the power you possess. Their lust for our women hasn't changed, and never will. You may hear, this is a man's world. That's a lie. Y'all run it. Look out for one another."

"Always." I smiled, patting my hip.

He winked, while Tipp was clueless to the gesture.

"Get on outta here. Get back here at a decent hour. Don't have me come lookin' for you. I ain't tryin' to catch another case."

Teague is a blessing to us. He stayed dropping jewels on us when he had the opportunity. Keeping us on point. Keeping that in mind, I didn't care what Cyn said. Niggaz had the bag, and I wanted to go get it. She'd fucked around and caught feelings. I think we all could tell she was dick struck. We got in the van, and Mula pulled off.

I said, "Now, before we get to this club! Is there anything anybody needs to tell me? I don't like surprises."

Sweets nudged her. "Yeah, Cyn? Speaking of the last time we kicked it with these niggaz."

# Chapter 16

## *SWEETS*

### *We Be on It*
### *New Year's Eve: 5 Months Prior*

The night was still young. Jeezo and The Gunnaz sat at tables surrounding Money and Honor. This wasn't Money's nor Honor's first time at Red Corvette, as though they'd made it seem. They'd visited occasionally when Money came to the Mil to check on his family. Everybody was chillin' poppin' champagne. They had a surprise for the youngsters. They'd called ahead of time and asked that we'd join them at the club. Of course, there were plenty of ladies in the building for them to choose from.

Money and Honor knew when it came to PYT we were on a whole 'nother level. D.J. Homer Blow had it jumpin'! He always fucked with Hip-Hop's finest. As if on cue, he spun *I Need Love*. A major cut off L.L.'s *Bigger And Deffer* album as we walked in. As you know, we're an all-female crew headed by none other than my sister Tasha. Better known as 2-Hood. Now a group of six, but that night we stepped in ten deep. Even niggaz there with their main thangz stopped and stared, but we were scoping the lick. We be on it.

"Damn! The whole clique bad!" one of the patrons yelled from the bar.

The ladies we'd brought with us were bad as fuck as well. The Gunnaz were in for a treat. Cyn is the only Puerto Rican out the crew. It seems as though Money fell in love the moment Hood introduced them.

One night, he and Honor came to Milwaukee to check on his sister Anna T. She'd given Money Tasha's number, being he'd said he wanted to check out the Mil's nightlife while he was here. Auntie knew Tasha was in the streets. Money never imagined that—that night, he'd be introduced to someone as beautiful as Cyn. No doubt, he loved his black women. He loved him some T.G. but there was something different about Cyn. Overall, what shined to him most was her personality. Her natural curly hair, her body and her skin tone also made her stand out from the rest. As we approached, Burner was the first to address us. Hand on his weapon, he extended his arm motioning us to stop.

"May I help you ladies? Sorry, ahem!" He cleared his throat. "How can I help you beautiful ladies?" He corrected himself, checkin' our sexy.

Bad bitches had him a lil nervous. Cyn smiled, and peeked around him at Re-Money, then back at him. She crossed her arms, then checked him.

She said, "Ask your boss, wait let me rephrase that for you, sweety. Ask your Boss—esss! Then, maybe! Just maybe we'll be able to help you." she was giving him all the attitude she could with her hands, neck and her eyes. She was still smiling, though.

"Burn! Be easy!" Honor roared. "These pretty young thangz come as a gift."

He laughed. "Ladies, meet The Young Gunnaz of the South," he introduced their young squad.

"Girrrl! You ain't tell us these niggaz had security! And they cute, too!" Pam said, snappin' her fingers and wavin' her hands in the air.

Lue said, "Mu—Mu, girl yo' ass is crazy. You need to quit-yo-shit, bitch."

Lue and Cyn walked pass Burn like runway models toward the tables Money and Honor occupied and sat on their laps. They were wearing these skin-tight leather pants that hugged every curve. Crossing their legs, they wasted no time giving their dudes passionate kisses. Deadly and the crew watched in awe for a few seconds, then quickly began giving their own personal introductions and offering seats.

"Boy, please! We ain't come up in here to be sittin' down! We came to dance," Pam said, as she grabbed Thorough and and pulled him to the dance floor.

Roxanne Shuntae blazed through the speakers causing the crowd to erupt. Sticks grabbed Tasha, and Studda grabbed my hand. We'd been eyeing each other since we'd stepped to their tables.

"Shit, I want some of this champagne." Jade, one of the extras we'd brought took a seat at the table with the bottles.

"Me too!" Rozlinn countered, grabbing the seat next to her. She was another extra.

Jeezo looked at Money and Honor with his eyebrows raised. He'd snagged Brianna and was ready to try to get to know her better.

"What's up, y'all good?" he asked.

They knew he wanted to getaway. Honor smiled.

He said, "We're thrilled Y.G.!" Meaning they were strapped.

"Go have fun! That's what we came for." Money grinned, running his hand across Cyn's thigh.

Fat Mack yelled, "Par-taaaay!"

We all stood to leave Money and Honor alone with Lue and Cyn. Deadly looked back and winked, as he strolled to the dance floor with somethin' sexy on both arms.

Money said, "Honor, check Deadly out. Nique gon' kill that boy."

He laughed, then yelled, "Y'all come back after a few songs! We'll have some more drinks over here."

"Yeah, cause y'all gon' need some shit." Jade was still gulpin' down champagne.

"Yo' drunk ass!" Lue said, as she and Cyn busted out laughing.

Jade's only reply was, "Um—hmm! Shoooot!"

She and Rozlinn got their guzzle on.

At this point, Money had been cheating on T.G. for about a year or so. He'd even went as far as gettin' an apartment in the Mil she didn't know about. Cyn had a key, but since Money was always gone she was rarely there.

"So, Money where you been, nigga?" Cyn asked.

"I've been workin', bae. We gotta eat, right?" he replied.

"You ain't been fuckin' no bitches, have you?"

"Nah, you know I love you." He smooched her lips. "You miss me?"

"You know I have. I need some. You stayin'?"

"Yeah. We can put the YGz in a hotel, or they can drive back. I'm with you, though." He kissed her again.

She said, "Good, cause I got something to tell you, Papi."

"You do, huh?" he replied, while unzipping her pants. He slid his hand inside to find her clit.

"Hmmm—hmmmmm!" she moaned, as he kissed her neck.

It was dark in the VIP section. You couldn't tell what was goin' on unless someone was really paying attention. Honor and Lue were also discussing plans for the night. It had been weeks since they'd seen each other, and she didn't hold her tongue.

"What up with some dick, nigga!" she spoke loud enough in his ear to emphasize she wouldn't be excepting *no* for an answer.

Just as he was about to respond, he noticed a group of men that seemed to be moving in their direction. Deadly and Burn had noticed as well. They made it back to the table before the men got within twenty feet, ready for war. Both Cyn and Lue had their backs to the crowd.

"Money! P's and Q's!" Honor yelled over the music.

In front of a coterie of about fifty men, was this short Hispanic lookin' muthafucka wearing a black suit and shades. There were a few other dudes with him, that looked Hispanic as well. The majority were black. The music screeched to a halt. The man leading the group toward Money and Honor said something to his men in Spanish. They all stood firm as he approached Deadly and Burn.

"Seven—Nineteen!" Deadly yelled the code for SG, letting the squad know that they may have to shoot it out.

The YG'z stood at attention spreading out and covering all exits. Thorough made his way through the crowd and back to the tables. He stood in back of Burn and Deadly, putting another body and two more guns between the big homies and the stranger. The Hispanic dude took off his shades. He seemed to be looking past the Gunnaz, and at Money and Cyn. He smiled.

"Babe—baby, bra?" It was hard for Cyn to speak, realizing who it was.

She couldn't believe her eyes. She covered her mouth on the verge of tears. She hadn't seen him in years. Standing up, she stepped away from Money's side. She stepped in front of the Gunnaz, happy things hadn't gotten out of hand.

As they spoke in Spanish, neither Money nor Honor knew what was being said. They were patiently waiting for the gibber-jabber's end.

Cyn said, "Los dos vestidos de negro son Los que tu tier queconoser." then she said, "Money, Honor, this is my baby brother, Kilo. Bruh, this is my man and his chief enforcer, Honor." She rushed her brother and held him tight. She'd missed him and was glad to see him.

"Thorough, I know you on your P's?" Honor spoke through his teeth like a ventriloquist.

Money stood to shake the hand Kilo extended in his direction as soldiers from both sides looked on. As they greeted each other with smiles, the music resumed. As Money returned to his seat, he grabbed Rough by his arm.

"You get all that?" he asked.

"Got it," he replied.

Honor was now standing to greet Kilo as well, though he didn't like it.

"Have a seat," Honor insisted as they shook hands.

Money said, "Have a drink."

"I'd love to. I see my sister has made wise choices in her selection of friends. Honor, Money, I love and respect them both," Kilo stated as he popped the cork on a bottle of Moet. He served himself and pulled up a chair.

"So do we," Honor replied.

"We love Kilo as well," Money said, pulling Cyn back into his lap. Her brother looked, but he didn't say shit. "Kilo, what else do you drink?" Money raised his hand to flag the waitress.

"Remy. That good shit," Kilo replied.

The waitress approached and Money ordered thirty bottles of Remy X0 and twenty more bottles of champagne. When she left, he said, "Rough, give that to Honor for me.

"Damn! Excuse me for a second. Let me holla at the guys real quick."

Mack and The Gunz were still on G-shit. Honor stood up and threw up one finger, signaling everything was good. Honor pulled Rough to the side to get the rundown on the conversation between Kilo and Cyn. Rough and Burn were both fluent in Spanish. Brooklyn had taught them well.

"Is this nigga who she says he is or what?" Honor questioned.

"I can't say for sure, but apparently so. When he approached us, he told the jawn that he didn't know she liked chocolate. Then he asked who we were. She told him to shut up, and that she'd seen him with chocolate on several occasions. Guess he likes the milk. She told him he could speak English, that we're good. That's when he asked her to introduce him. She told him the two in black are the ones you need to meet. Yo, you know what it is with me, B. If you think these bitches on some setup shit, we can—"

"Nah, we good. I was trippin'. It sounded like he called us some niggaz."

"Aw, you mean when she said negro? That means black."

"Round up the squad. We got some more drinks comin'. I don't know about y'all. But, tonight, I'm gettin' me some pussyy!" They gave each other dap.

Honor made it back to the tables in the middle of another conversation between Cyn and her brother.

"So, little brother, how have you been?" she asked.

"Come on, sis. You know me, I always good." His English was still a little off.

"I haven't seen you in a while. I heard you'd gone back to Philly when you disappeared from the island. What brings you back this way?" she asked.

"Business, and a little pleasure." He smiled. "You know I have to see Mama and Papa. Also, never forget." He wagged his finger at her. "Just because you don't see me, doesn't mean I don't see you."

"Well, I'm glad you're here. I can bring in the New Year and share this special moment with you."

Everybody was back at the tables. All her PYTs and all the YGz. We were drinking, smoking, and talking shit when Cyn stood up and grabbed a bottle of champagne. She stepped in the center of us all.

"Hold up!" she yelled, hoisting the bottle in the air. "Hold up everybody! Hold up y'all! Everybody! Ev-ry-bod-deee!"

Finally, we all paused. All eyes were on Cyn. She had our attention.

She said, "Everybody pour up with me! Come on, stop lookin' at me like that! I wanna tell y'all somethin' dang!" After all our flutes were filled, she continued, "I can't believe what I'm about to announce, but it's true. Wow, tonight is such a special night. We're all here together, kickin' it. I've got my brother here. My man. My girlz! Y'all my sistahs, y'all know I love each and every one of y'all."

We were all wondering what the hell was goin' on as we stood in a circle holding up our drinks.

She said, "I can't drink with y'all tonight, so y'all take this one to the head for me. I was gon' wait and tell Money later, when we were alone. But since we've got so many here that we both love. I may as well do it now. Everybody look around. Go ahead! I'm serious! Take a good look, because, our families are about to become one."

We all looked at each other. More than likely thinking the same thing. *What the hell is she talkin' about?* We didn't have a clue.

Then she said it, "I'm pregnant!"

"Oh! Ohhh! Shit!" Money's friends cheered.

People were downing their drinks and giving each other their signature handshake while also giving Money and Cyn hugs.

We were speechless. Clearly Money was as shocked as we were.

Hood was pissed, though she masked it with a smile. My mind drifted back to the day she'd called and asked us if we wanted to kick it with some niggas from Racine. Damn, I hadn't expected no shit like this.

*Mm-mmm! And who is this brother of hers?* Sipping my drink, I couldn't help but wonder.

I knew damn well she hadn't ever mentioned him to us! I couldn't even get mad though. We'd kept a gang of shit from her in the past.

*Payback's a bitch, but me and this hoe needed to talk!* "A'ight Cyn! That's good shit!" I yelled. As she glanced in my direction, I raised my glass. "Congrats, bitch!" I laughed. "Happy New Year!"

## Chapter 17

### *BRI*

We needed to hurry up and have this meeting. To keep traffic at a minimum at Hood's, that Monday we held a session at my house. I knew my momma would be working a double, so we had all night to see what else if anything we could learn about these niggaz Lue and Cyn been fuckin' with. So far, all we had was they got money, loved the finer things as we do and one of 'em had put a baby in our sister. But what part of the game is this?

Cyn shocked us all with this shit! *Pregnant?* They were supposedly on their way here an hour ago. Me, Hood, Mula, and Sweets were waiting on their asses. They'd spent the entire weekend laid up at a Hotel with them fools, as if one baby on the way wasn't enough.

"Ooh, I can't wait! She got her nerve, don't she?" Hood paced the floor.

We lined the sofa watching an episode of The women of Brewster Place that my mother had dubbed to VHS.

"Sure do!" Sweets said. "You see my face when she said it?"

"You see mine?" Mula replied.

After that, it was just a whole bunch of chatter that none of us understood. Cause we were all trying to talk at the same damn time. That's until we heard the thuds of car doors slamming in the driveway. Then the chirp of an alarm.

Hood said, "They're here! Everybody, just calm down." Being that she was more upset than any of us, she said, "Let me have a seat myself. Before I mess around and snap." She'd sat at the dining room table as I got up to open the door.

"Come on in, hoes," I greeted them as they walked up on the porch.

They came in, and I shut the door behind them. The vibe was completely off, and they felt it in the air.

Lue said, "Ooh, it's cold!" She started coming out of her coat.

"It's all quiet in here. That movie can't be that damn good. What up?" Cyn tried to follow up.

Sweets said, "Yeah, what's up?"

"You tell us!" Hood barked. "Y'all down there in Racine fuckin'! Done had ya selves a hot summer, huh?"

"I said, "Yeah, Cyn, how could you keep this from us?"

"How far along are you?" Sweets asked.

Before she could answer, Mula hit her with the hard one.

"Was that shit at the Vette a show? Or have you really fallen for this, nigga? You let him go up in you raw?"

Cyn was stuck, she said, "Dang, can I sit down? I-I can explain."

Strangely, Lue ain't have shit to say. At least not at that point. She just sighed and took a seat at the table across from Hood. I remained standing, while Cyn took the seat Hood pointed out for her on the couch next to Sweets and Mula.

"Go head. You've got the floor. Please do explain this shit," Hood told her with a cold stare.

She said, "I'm a few months. I thought y'all would be happy for me. I-I didn't plan on gettin' pregnant. It just happened."

Sweets said, "Girl, how many months is a few?"

"Three and a half. Look, I apologize for it coming to y'all as it did. I should've came to y'all first."

"Humph! I guess. If you like it, I love it," Sweets said with a smile as she rubbed her belly.

"And dude?" Mula looked over at her. "You the one?"

"Good question—" she paused. "I don't know y'all. But spending so much time with him, there's some feelings there. This doesn't mean I haven't been on my job if that's what you're asking."

Hood leaned in, resting her elbows on her knees. She said, "Hold up y'all. That's exactly what we're askin'. You ready to run everything down?"

"Yeah. Why not?"

"Well, we're listening. Like I said, you got the floor. Lue, I see you over there. Get ready, cause yo' lil ass is next." Hood folded her arms as she leaned back and got comfortable. She said, "Go 'head Cyn. Nah, wait. Mula, you got that?"

"You know what? Damn I forgot—" Mula paused, then she smiled. She reached inside her hoodie. "This shit here a getcha higher than Jordan." She pulled out a half ounce of weed.

Hood said, "You can start, by telling us about this brother of yours."

"I knew my brother poppin' up like that would raise some questions. Now, y'all wanna know where he came from, and why I hadn't mentioned him, right?"

"You damn skippy, bitch. Run that shit?" Sweets said.

"Well, I was gon' eventually tell y'all. But the first person I had to sit down with was Money. That way my child's father would know a lil' more about where I came from. Kilo is a hustler's dream come true. Born in the mean streets of Puerto Rico, survival instincts emerged at a very young age. They have to, coming from where I'm from. Niggas think they're gettin' money.

"That lil' bread ain't shit compared to my brother's status. Small things to a giant. My brother's real name is Carlos. Kilo was originally the name of his mentor. He was one of the most powerful kingpins to ever run the island. When his name is mentioned, there's as much respect today as there was thirty years ago. Kilo wasn't just a hustler. He was also known to be a stone-cold killer."

# Chapter 18

## *CYN*
## *Comin' From Where I'm From*

One afternoon, Carlos was kickin' it with his childhood friend Lamone when Kilo pulled up in a red Ferrari. He jumped out of the car carrying a chrome briefcase in one hand, while talking on a cellular. Though my brother had heard stories about his legend, he'd never seen him in person. He had no idea that the man we'd heard so many stories about was right there in front of him about to walk in the bodega across the street.

*"Whoa, you see that car? Who is that?" he asked his friend.*

*"Oh, that's Kilo," Lamone replied, like he was a nobody. As if Kilo was some ordinary Joe.*

*"You talkin' about The Kilo?" he questioned.*

*"Yeah, Kilo. I surely doubt there's another on the island," Lamone replied.*

*"You know him?" Bro asked.*

*"Yeah. Everybody does." Lamone looked my brother like he was stupid, using his hand to shade his eyes from the sun.*

*"You lie! You don't know him!" Carlos shoved him playfully.*

*"Oh, yeah? You wanna meet him?" he asked, holding up the paper bag he'd been carrying.*

*My bro hadn't paid attention to shit.*

*"What the fuck is that?" he asked.*

*"Just be cool, I'll show you. Watch this."*

*As Kilo exited the store moments later, Lamone called out to him, "Kiloii Valla Papi!"*

*The boss looked over and smiled. He walked over to them, and Lamone handed him the bag. Kilo shook his hand, and then Carlos's.*

*He said, "Gotta go, I'm in a hurry."*

*He walked back over and got in the Ferrari. He then called out to Lamone, "Lamone! Wait for my call." Then he sped off.*

Carlos was stunned. He couldn't believe he'd actually shaken the hand of the man that seemed to have the world in his palm. It was then, that he started badgering his friend about the contents of the brown paper bags he'd seen him with week after week. Lamone was dressed like the average twelve-year old kid. Never would one imagine what he told Carlos.

He said, he dropped Kilo fifty thousand or more per week. My brother wondered how he could be managing so much cash. He said that all the rumors we'd heard about Kilo were true. Anybody that was somebody on the island, answered to Kilo in some form or fashion. My brother wanted in. Lamone promised he'd deliver the message.

A week later, Lamone showed up at Carlos' house, carrying another brown paper bag. He asked Carlos to walk to the store with him. It was the same store where Carlos had seen Kilo for the first time. This time there was no red sports car. Kilo arrived in a black big body Benz. He parked across the street and got out. He strolled over to the boys. Lamone handed Kilo the bag of money.

From the time Kilo exited the Benz, he seemed to be eyeing Carlos, as if he was sizing him up. Kilo knew he had to have heard about all the murders his name was tied to. The amputations of hands, legs, and feet of those who'd stole as little as twenty dollars from him. The many decapitations of his rivals. The bombings of houses and cars, blowing up entire families.

It's said he'd even thrown family members that had crossed him off the cliffs of La Perla to be devoured in the shark infested waters. There are hundreds of bodies that'll never be found at the hands of Kilo. He wanted to see if the young boy was intimidated by his presence, if he showed any signs of weakness, or fear he would have nothing to do with him.

*"Who is this the kid you speak so highly of Lamone?" he questioned.*

*"This is, Papi. He's the same one that was with me before. We've come up together."*

*"You vouch for him?" he asked, still eyeing Carlos.*

*He didn't blink. "Yes, with my life."*

*"Okay," Kilo replied.*

*He turned his back, walked over to the Benz, and jumped in. He threw the bag in the back seat like it was garbage. He then retrieved something from the passenger seat. He walked back over to them with a cell phone. It was huge, like the ones you'd see on an old army flick. It had the big, thick fold down antenna. He handed it to Carlos.*

*He said, "Carlos, nobody—I mean, nobody knows the number to this phone but me. Wait for my call. Okay? You stick with Lamone. He'll show you everything."*

*"Okay," Carlos replied.*

*"Lamone, we talk later. Wait for my call," that said, Kilo left.*

*A month went by, and the phone never rang. Then, one night, suddenly it did.*

*He answered, "Hello."*

*"Carlos?" Kilo said very calmly.*

*"Yeah!" he replied.*

*"It's me. You ready?"*

*"Yeah. I'm ready." Carlos said.*

*"Good, so am I."*

"Being that he made moves faster than any worker his age, Kilo took an instant liking to him. They were together so much, people thought he was Kilo's son. They started calling him, Lil Kilo. Kilo taught him everything. They'd made millions together. Sadly, ten years into their partnership, Kilo was killed by one of his henchmen. Carlos has been holding the name down ever since."

# Chapter 19

## *HOOD*

Bri thought she heard a muffler outside that sounded a tad too familiar, she got up. "Hold up y'all, that sound like my mama car."

"Well, what happened, Cyn?" Mula asked as Bri glanced out the window.

"Bri said wait," Cyn replied.

"Fuck that! Keep goin'." Sweets waved her off, wanting to hear more.

"Oh shit! That is my momma! She musta got off early!" cried Bri.

We paused for a second. Then everybody started scrambling. Lue ran upstairs. Cyn went toward the kitchen. Me and Sweets headed for the bathroom. I don't know what was up with Mula; that ass was stuck.

I made my way out of the living room, moving at a fast pace. I told Bri, "You better spray somethin'!," But it was too late. Ms. Hines was already coming through the door.

"Brianna, why is this here car in my— Aw, hell naw!"

"I know, Ma! I was finna spray," Bri tried to protest. She'd finally grabbed the air freshener.

"What I tell y'all lil' asses about smokin' that dope in my house?" Ms. Hines snapped. "Get out!"

"It's just weed, it ain't dope, Ma. You buggin'?"

"All of y'all get out. Ain't no need of you hiding, cause I know you're here and I know you hear me! Now I better not have to say it again. Brianna, that means you too! Take yo' lil' hardheaded ass with 'em. Sittin' up in here smokin'! Y'all gon' wind up bein' a bunch of crack heads."

"But Ma!"

"Girl, you better getcha tail on outta here!"

"What?"

She didn't have to tell me twice. I was waitin' on my opportunity as soon as she'd announced she smelled that weed we'd blown. I already knew what time it was. She musta gotten on Cyn's ass about her driveway. Cause by the time she came out, the rest of us had already hopped in the van with Mula. I was ridin' shotty.

"Mu, hit the horn real quick." I rolled my window. "I know she see us. Aye, Cyn!"

"What up?" She turned around.

"Ahhh! Yo' ass got caught up, huh? Yo, she illin' or what?" I laughed, lookin' toward the house.

"Whatchu think?" she replied.

"I told you about that driveway. Park the BM and hop that lil' pretty ass in here with us. We going to my crib, fuck it."

We did just that.

# Chapter 20

## *MONEY*
## *Plugged*

To me, it was a pleasure to hear Kilo's story. To know where he'd come from was intriguing to me. He'd treated me and Honor like family ever since the night we'd met. We'd discussed his business on several occasions during the six months he was in town. Everything he shared with me, I told Honor. He didn't believe half of it. He thought it was all bullshit.

One night, about a year later, I got a call from Kilo.

The only thing he said was, "My sister needs a vacation, bring her home." It was the code we'd put a stamp on before he left Milwaukee.

He was finally ready to allow me into his world. We booked the next flight to Puerto Rico.

True to his mentor's legacy, when we arrived at the Ritz Carlton on the island, and were comfortably relaxing in our suites the phone rang.

When I answered, the only thing I heard was, "Wait for my call." The line went dead.

I smiled, remembering his story. Cyn took us all over the island. They had no idea I was really there on business. I'd told her I simply wanted to see where she was from. Our first day there, me and Honor rented motorcycles and rode Cyn and Lue around. The following day, we turned the bikes in for Ferraris, which ran us about fifteen thousand a day. Honor rented a red one. Mine was white and we raced each other, while Cyn and Lue screamed hysterically in the passenger seats.

We made sharp turns, burning rubber as we hit top speeds of one hundred and eighty miles per hour. We were driving as if we'd been there a thousand times. Days passed, and we were having a ball. We'd swam in the ocean, shopped and dined-in at the island's finest restaurants. We went dancing every night. I would've never imagined that they got it in so hard over there. The women are so exotic. It was like a dream. Everybody seemed so nice. Women approached, speaking in Spanish. They had to be thinking we were Puerto Ricans as well. Being that we didn't understand, me and Honor would just nod and say, "What's up?" in English.

It was a Sunday, June 16th, around 10:45 at night. Me and Cyn were relaxing in the Jacuzzi after three long hours of fuckin' and suckin'. The phone rang. It was Kilo. The call I'd been waiting on the entire trip.

"You ready?" he asked.

"Always," I replied.

"I'll pick you up in an hour outside in front. Just you, though. Leave HG. You're safe with me."

"Bet."

"One hour."

"I'm there." I hung up.

I got out of the jacuzzi and headed for the shower.

"Where you going, Papi?" Cyn asked. "Who was that, Honor?" She had her eyes closed letting the jets hit her body.

"That was your brother. I don't know how he knew we were here, but he wants to take me out for drinks. You cool?"

"Yeah, go head. I'm glad y'all connecting. I'll see you when you get back. I'm about to lay down anyway." She yawned. "Tell Kilo I said, *"Make sure he makes his way to see me before we leave."*

"I will."

I got up from the edge of the Jacuzzi and went and got in the shower. I got dressed, and a half hour later, Kilo was pulling in front of the Ritz in a Navy-blue Range. I hopped in. He drove a while. Soon we were miles away from the highly populated areas. It was to a point where other cars looked like ants in the distance. The roads became dense and narrow. Finally, we ended up at what appeared to be a deserted beach.

Parking and getting out, we opened the hatchback of the Rover and grabbed two blankets and a flashlight. He'd thrown me the blankets as we walked toward the sand. The stars and the moon lit the night's sky. The ocean repeatedly roared like a lion that weighed a sextillion ton.

He said, "I know, you gotta be thinking. What in the hell are we doing out here?"

He was right. "Exactly."

I hadn't brought my thriller. For a moment I thought this mutha-fucka might be trying to kill me!

"Well, this is the part I never told you about," he said as he walked ahead.

We were now on the sand, walking toward the water. He turned, took a blanket from me. He spread it out on the sand and took a seat. I was confused.

"Have a seat, guy. Do get comfortable. I've had a long day. I need to close my eyes for a minute." He handed me the flashlight. "Hold this." He laid back and closed his eyes. He said, "I need you to watch the ocean for me."

I spread my blanket and sat a few feet away from him, trying to figure this shit out.

He said, "Let me know when you see a light flash out there, okay? It's going to flash three times. Wake me as soon as you see that a'ight."

"A'ight," I replied.

He dozed off, I was growing tired as well. I'd been watching the ocean's waves for about two hours when I finally spotted the first flash.

"Kilo! Aye, Kilooo!" I shook him awake.

He hopped to his feet. "How many flashes? How many, Money!"

"Three!" I replied.

"*Three?* Three flashes. Okay."

He grabbed the flashlight from me and flashed it toward the ocean three times, then turned and flashed it three times behind us. All of a sudden these camouflaged trucks I'd never noticed started pulling up from every direction. Soon after, a vessel came into sight. There were at least ten trucks about a hundred and fifty armed men. They let the ramp down and all I heard was the chatter of Spanish in the air. They'd unloaded barrel after barrel of pure coke and Heroin into the trucks, taking all the ship's cargo. To me, the shit was unreal.

"Don't worry about the police!" he said. "You're looking at them. They're all on payroll, from the military to the new boots." He smiled, rubbing his hands together. "Welcome to Puerto Rico, ha-haa!" He laughed.

We followed the trucks back to the warehouse where the shipments were unloaded. There was so much product stacked in rows, that I had to be looking at some tons. The shit was damn near stacked to the ceiling. I couldn't believe my eyes.

He said, "Money, you ready to live up to your name?"

"Shit, I thought I was! But after seeing what I've seen, I'm just a pawn trying to make it across the board."

"May your queen protect you. Don't worry, I take good care of you. You just make sure you take good care of my sister and my niece."

"I'll go to the end of the earth for 'em," I replied.

He said, "I'm going to make sure your hands are good. Let's go. The sun is about to rise.

We switched vehicles. We hopped in his black Porsche that was parked inside the warehouse along with a variety of luxury cars. We'd left there tailed by his security team. They drove two black vans.

Forty-five minutes later, the sun was shining bright. We'd arrived at his estate. It sat behind a huge iron fence, with a huge *F* in the center. The mansion was humongous. It was clear he'd spent a small fortune on the landscaping alone. It was flawless. He said it was done by a Nancy Powers. She'd done a helluva job. I could only dream this big.

He said the home was designed by the great architect Frank Gehry. It sat on 57 acres and was just one of many he owned. Inside, everything was designed by Clive Christian. He said the kitchen, lounge, and bedroom alone ran him a lil' over a half mil. It had cast iron seats leading to the lawn, and Blue stone coping surrounding the koi pond, his shit was plush. Out back he had a lap pool, and a

Jacuzzi. Armed men patrolled the grounds. Security cameras were everywhere. He'd come a long way since his *Oliver Twist* days in Monte Hatillo.

We sat outside by the pool at a dining table in bamboo chairs imported from Lhasa, as his beautiful maid served us breakfast. It was time to talk business.

"So, Money, how many bricks do you think you can handle, Papa?"

I put my fork down and dabbed the corners of my mouth with my handkerchief.

"Right now. Just let me get twenty of each. I wanna see how shit works out. I ain't never fucked with that horse before. But that bitch Cocoa. She'll be gone in no time. Triple the profit."

Okay, both, it is. The same way we discussed nineteen thousand fifty-five hundred for the girl and seventy-five thousand for the boy. Since you're new to Black T this first round is on consignment. Cool?"

"That's cool. My only question to you is, how am I supposed to get all this shit to the crib?" I asked taking a bite of my toast, with the homemade strawberry preserves.

"Don't worry about that, I got that covered. You just be at O'Hare when I tell you to. Some ladies from my circle will greet you. Some of them will be flight attendants, but don't be alarmed by the uniforms. I also got the airport security paid off."

"A'ight, make it happen then. I'm ready."

"Okay. But first I'm going to need yours, and Honor's social security cards, and IDs. I've already checked to be sure you are who you say you are. The thing is there's going to be a lot of money at stake. Wouldn't want you disappearing on me. This way my people can track you anywhere on the planet. Understand?"

"Cool, that ain't no problem. I understand."

"Good, I'll have everything copied, and back to you before you leave. But, for now, let's toast. To our partnership, friendship, and our bond. To you, me, and your boy Honor.

"To money, Honor, and Kilo." I raised my glass.

He was holding down Puerto Rico, North Philly, Milwaukee. He wanted Racine. He let it be known a hit squad was always ready to clean shit up, if anything got in the way of that paper. It's about to get real ugly in lil Raycilla with the prices we gettin' it for, the takeover is evident. We ain't gotta attempt to roll over niggaz. When the prices get low, and the product is pure wars begin."

Kilo was 5'6, a Miami bred lookin' ass nigga. In his eyes you saw murder. From a distance, you saw cash. He was short, but his reach is long.

# Chapter 21

## *Caught Up*

Back at home the sun rose and fell again. Me and Honor had another pick-up and drop scheduled for this afternoon. Kilo always had us drop the money off in the Mil before heading to O'Hare to pick up the product. This day was no different, except when I told my girl I was heading to Milwaukee for the weekend, she snapped. She'd grown suspicious of all my trips out of town on business. She'd suspected that I'd been cheating, and now she had proof. T.G. decided she'd let shit slide long enough. Today in our living room, she'd be heard.

"Laureece I'm sick of your bullshit! You ain't never here with me and your fuckin' son! All I ever hear is, *"I gotta do this! I gotta do that! I gotta handle this business!"* We are your fuckin' business! And who you been fuckin'? Cause you sure as hell ain't been fuckin' me!"

"Girl, I have been! Look, you trippin'. I ain't been fuckin' nobody."

"You know what? It sounded like you was about to say you been fuckin' me. But then you had to think about it, huh? When's the last time you hit this pussy, huh?" She walked up on me.

I musta looked like I was trying to calculate some shit in my head, so she answered the question for me, "It's been two months and some! Since when have we not fucked every day? Two and three times a day? Unless we couldn't because of my cycle? Nicca, you got me fucked up! I know you been fuckin' around on me! Who is it! Who is she, Laureece?" She swung on me. I caught the blow and grabbed her before she could swing again. "I hate yo' ass!" Tears run down her face as she struggled to break free from my grasp. "Let me go!" she screamed, jerking away from me. "I had your muthafuckin' junior! And this how you gon' do me! Me, Money! Who is this bitch!"

"What bitch? I ain't been fuckin' around with nobody but you. Damn, calm down. You gon' wake Gee up."

T.G. is beautiful. Like a mixture of *Alicia Keys and Lauren London.* She'd have no problem holding her own standing next to some of the world's finest today. She knew I was lying. I guess my body language said it all.

"You can't even look at me. Y—you know what? Fuck you, gon' where you goin'!" She marched upstairs, leaving me there with a decision to make.

I was wondering if I should leave. Or stay and try to fix things at home? I'd failed to realize that I'd been neglecting the crib. I'd indeed been spending more of my time in the Mil with Cyn. I hadn't counted T.G. as one that would pay attention to the changes in my routine, as long as I kept her laced with the finer things. I was wrong, she had. All the money in the world couldn't make up for the love and companionship she was missing.

At that very moment, I knew she hated the fact that she loved me. I gave her a few minutes before I went up after her. I was hoping she would calm down so we could talk before I left. I knew she didn't deserve this foul treatment and I coulda loved her so much better. Still upset, I found her packing her bags. She wasn't taking time to fold it, as she stuffed her shit in any bag she could put her hands on.

"Hold on! Where you going?"

"Why? Does it matter, huh? Does it? It's obvious you need to get your priorities straight. But if you really need to know, me and Gee goin' to my momma's house. Don't try to stop me, cause I don't even wanna hear it." She sniffed and wiped her tears away.

"Damn, you comin' back ain't you? How much shit you gon' take?"

"That's a good question. I don't know how much more of your bullshit I can stand. So, I don't l know how long I'ma be."

"Terry, stop playin' now." I laughed and tried to take some of the clothes out of her hands.

"Move, Laureece! Ain't nobody playin' with you! Now gon' handle yo' business! You definitely got something to handle. You better tell whatever hoe you been fuckin' that it's over! I don't play, I'm too fine to come second to whoever she is."

"Terry, I ain't fuckin'—"

"Laureece stop lying! See, that's why I'm gone."

"I'm not lying to you!" I pleaded my case.

She dropped her clothes on the bed and got in my face. She pointed her finger at me, emphasizing every word as she bounced and rolled her neck like only an angry black woman could.

"You're not lying, right now! You ain't lyin'! You done? Okay, who's Cynthia then, huh?" she questioned.

"I—I," I stuttered.

"I-I-I my ass! You sounding like the lil nigga that work for you! Who is Cyn-thi—ah! Money, you caught nicca! Yeah, you forgot you send me to pay all the bills around this bitch! Yup, all the late-night calls when you thought I was sleep. Mm-hm!" She nodded.

"I got the number right off the phone bill. The funny thing is when I called the bitch and asked her how she knew you? She said, *"You're her man!"* She picked up her clothes and started back stuffing bags. "Ain't that some shit, Money? Now, what you got to say, Mr. I—ain't-been-fuckin'? Me and Ms. Cynthia had a long ass talk, three o'clock this morning. This the part that kills me, though. The bitch said she's havin' yo' baby! I should've thrown some hot grits on yo' ass! What up? I can't hear you now, Money."

I wanted badly to hear that she was still in love with me. That she wasn't leaving. Even if it was far from the truth, she wanted me to tell her everything she'd heard was a lie.

"I'm sorry, I never meant to hurt you, bae," that was all I was able to muster.

"Oh!" She laughed. "Now you're sorry, huh? Laureece, just leave like you were about to. I don't even wanna see you right now."

"Baby, look." I reached for her, but she brushed me off.

She looked at me, she wanted to hit me, to hurt me any way that she could, but she knew she couldn't win like that. I was caught. There would be no lying my way out of this one. She was my first love. There was no explanation for my betrayal. She was heart-broken and couldn't hide it. She was still in tears when we heard a horn outside. I knew it had to be Honor. The moves we had to make couldn't be made without me. Timing was all fucked up.

"Come here, girl." I pulled her into my arms and tried to kiss her, but she turned her head in anger.

"Move! Don't touch me!"

I managed to give her a peck on the cheek before she broke free. The horn blew again. I told her I loved her and promised to make things right when I got back. But how could I? I left. She came to the window and watched as I got in the passenger's seat of Honor's black Fleetwood. As we pulled off, she picked up the phone.

# Chapter 22

## *HONOR*

### *Ridin' Dirty*
### *Three Days Later*

It was Monday, 12:45 p.m. Deadly and I were tailing Money and Jeezo as we pulled off the exit in Racine County. Money was driving his 1988 Chevy Camaro, and it was packed with bricks. I followed closely making sure no police were able to get behind him. I noticed a Sheriff's squad car sitting in the parking lot of The Marriott to our left. As soon as we passed, he jumped behind us. As we headed West past Case High School toward 16$^{th}$ Street, I peeped another squad car speeding behind the first. Then there was another, and another. There were now four cars behind us as we turned onto 16$^{th}$, heading South toward Green Bay Road. Then, the bright lights lit us up.

"Fuck!" I roared. "These muthafuckas pullin' us over!"

Seeing all that was going on behind us caused me to breakout in a cold sweat. I knew Money had enough dope in the car to put us away for life. Money continued to cruise doing the speed limit as I pulled over. I sighed a breath of relief, seeing all the squads had pulled behind me and Deadly in the Lac. As Money and Jeezo headed around the bend in the road, I'm sure they'd took notice to how the police jumped out. This was no ordinary traffic stop. As I looked through my rearview, I could tell by the numbers, and by the way they'd got down on us, it could only mean one or two things. Scenario one, me or Deadly had a warrant. Two, somebody was snitching, knowing we'd gone to re-up.

While shotguns, police issued .9mm and .38s were aimed at us, an officer projected his voice over the loudspeaker, "Driver and passenger! Let me see your hands!"

We both complied, putting our hands on the ceiling.

"Driver, using your left hand! Turn off the engine!"

I slowly reached through the steering wheel, turned the ignition and put my hand back up.

"Damn, dog. We both double breasted in this bitch," Deadly said sourly.

"I know," I replied. "But don't move. One of 'em at your window."

Deadly turned his head slightly to the right but saw nothing. "He's at the back window outside your peripheral. He's pointing a shotty at your head. Don't move, G."

"Passenger! With your left hand! Slowly open the door!"

Deadly opened the door, and suddenly the officer I saw was at him screaming, "Hands—hands—hands—hands!" the pig yelled over loudspeaker, "Now! Passenger, exit the vehicle, face South! Do not turn around!"

Deadly got out the car. Out of the corner of his eye, he could still see the barrel of the shotgun that was trained at his head.

"Now, walk backward to the sound of my voice! Come on back! Back—back—back! Now stop! Get on your knees and cross your ankles!" Deadly did as he was told.

"Now lay flat on your stomach spreading your arms away from your body!"

He laid down as commanded and immediately felt the pain of several officer's body weight on his frame. They twisted his arms as if they had every intention of breaking them. Then frisked his body.

"Where the dope at, boy?" one asked.

When another felt one of the thrillaz, the punk ass, rednecks went crazy. "Gun—gun—gun—gun!" the other officers had their guns pointed at me screaming, "Don't move! Don't you move motherfucker! Don't move!"

They were itching for either of us to give them a reason to kill us.

Then, there was the loudspeaker again, "Driver! Do not move! I repeat, don't move!"

They had the Wood surrounded. One officer snatched my door open, while two others dragged me out onto the pavement. I was pissed. They were handling me real rough.

Stretched out on the ground, I yelled, “What the fuck y’all stop me for!”

“We got an anonymous tip that this vehicle would be transporting drugs, you fuckin’ monkey! Now close your mouth before I kick you in it!” one replied.

“Gun—gun-gun! We’ve got two more!” another yelled.

They slapped the cuffs on me and threw me in the back of a squad car. I watched as the K-9 went to work, sniffing around the whip. More and more cars arrived. Racine, black and whites as well as Detectives.

*This stankin’ ass German Shepherd done jumped in my backseat!* I thought, shaking my head.

“So, this is it?" I heard one of the officers’ question with a smile. “Honor one, huh?” This piqued my suspicion, since the officer had just arrived.

“Yup, right there on the plates. Read ‘em and weep. We’ve got two .9s and two .45 caliber pistols off the suspects. Hopefully, the tip we received is good and we’ll find the drugs the caller said was coming in. Supposed to be big.”

*What the fuck! Who coulda called in on us?* I thought.

***

Fifteen minutes later, at 30 miles per hour, Money and Jeezo had finally made it to the spot on Elm. The close encounter with the law had them shook. They just wanted to get their minds right.

As they got out, Money said, “Fuck that! That shit was too close. We’ll just leave it in the car until it gets dark. Later, we’ll pull it in the garage and bust it down.”

“Yeah, that was close,” Jeezo replied. “We can keep an eye on it from the spot. I’ll tell the squad to be on their Ps.”

“Yeah, do that. Right now, I gotta see what’s up with Deadly and Honor. I know they found the thrillaz.”

# Chapter 23

## *DEADLY*
## *Booked*

I was fingerprinted and booked on two counts of possession of a firearm. During the process, I was being transferred from one holding cell to another. Looking ahead, I saw Honor standing amongst a few other men inside the steel think tank. It was good to see a familiar face. The guard escorting me opened the door to the bullpen and pushed me in. He slammed the door behind me. I greeted the big homie with the one, as we shook up.

"Yo'! What the fuck's up, Honor, man? You know somebody called in on us, right?" I questioned.

He said, "Yeah, I heard something of the sort while the crackers had me stretched out on the concrete with pistols to my dome. I ain't know if I should've believed it or not. How you hear about it?"

"While I was in the squad, I heard one of the Jakes mention it to another. Pussies was laughing like it was some kind of joke or some shit."

"Well, I know they're pissed that they ain't find no dope. The good news is you'll be out within a few hours. Money gon' see to it. The bad is, I'm out on parole, so I'm facing revocation. Make sure you put 'em up on what's being said about this so-called tip. Once I retain a lawyer, I'll see what I can do from this side of the fence.

"Damn, Honor. How much time you got on paper?"

"Two years, tacking on another mandatory eighteen months or so for these new charges! I'll be home in three. Maybe three in a half."

The jingle of keys caught everybody's attention. The guard was opening the door again.

"Cox! Windell Cox, you're heading to four B! Let's go!"

Honor stood up. "A'ight. That's me lil' dog. Take it easy on 'em out there, young."

"Come on, man. You already know. No mercy, man. No mercy." I laughed, as we showed love with a handshake.

"Okay, YG, I'll be in touch." Honor stepped outta the tank.

The door slammed shut. Two hours later, I awoke to my name being called.

"Webb! Webb! Marian Webb!" the sheriff yelled.

I see a fat, unattractive female guard standing in the doorway of the bullpen.

"What?"

"Your bond has been posted. You're being released. Get up, bring your blanket and your cup!"

# Chapter 24

## *HONOR*

As soon as I got to the pod, I dropped my blanket and my toiletries in the cell I was assigned to and jumped on the phone. After I dialed the number, the pre-recorded operator said the same shit she'd been saying for years. "Please state your name after the beep."

"Honor."

"All calls, other than properly placed attorney calls may be monitored and recorded. Please hold." The phone rung three times before I finally got an answer. I could hear Trish's voice on the other end as she excepted the call. I smiled.

"Hello."

"You have a collect call from, Honor. An inmate in the Racine County Jail. To accept charges, press one. To decline press—thank you for using Viacom. You may start your conversation now."

"Hello!"

"Hey. Trish, baby, what's—"

"Nigga, please! Don't baby me!" I was puzzled.

"What? What's wrong?"

"I just cut up all yo' shit! That's what's wrong for one! I ain't move in with you to be going through all this bullshit! Yo' ass thought you was slick, huh!"

"Baby, wha—what's wrong? What you talking about?"

"T.G. called me the other day telling me some bullshit about yo' boy Money! And sure as shit stank, I put two and two together! Hoes of a feather flock together!" I dropped my head.

She said, "Of a feather! Checked the muthafuckin' phone bills! And here go the bitch number! So, yeah, I called. Being that I'm usually the only one using this phone. I'm wondering who the hell could be placing all these calls at two and three in the gotdamn morning! And all day while I'm at work!"

"Trish, calm down! Why you hollerin'?" I felt like everybody in the pod could hear her chipmunking through the phone.

"Fuck that! Guess what?"

"What, bae?"

"The bitch Lucinda answered! We talked!"

"And what y'all talk about, baby?" I asked with a bit of sarcasm in my voice.

She said, "You muthafucka! And, since you think everything's so damn funny. I'm the one that called in on yo' sorry ass! Don't drop the soap, nigga! Laugh at that!" She hung up.

"Trish—I know this bitch didn't jus—Trish!" I was heated.

I dialed the number again but got no answer. There was nothing I could do but prepare for this court battle. As bad as I wanted her dealt with, I knew I would've been the first suspect. After all, the conversation had been recorded.

Kilo got wind of the jam I was in a few weeks later. He sent one of Philly's top Criminal Defense attorneys that money could buy. Oscar McMillian was well respected and known for his devotion to his clients. He was well worth his asking price of $30,000. Though he hated Wisconsin's, Just—Us, Back Of The Bus, slave trade tactics as much as any lawyer in the country outside of the state, he took the case. It was one of many business ventures that he'd taken on account of Kilo.

Weeks behind on the case, he flew in and got straight to work. He'd filed a motion that not only got the charges thrown out on my behalf, but Deadly's as well. Using case law well established by the Federal Courts, the judge presiding over the case had no choice but to grant the defense's motion to suppress and dismiss. Citing an anonymous tip isn't sufficient enough evidence to conduct a stop and search, deeming the evidence tainted in its process. This was definitely a relief for me and the crew.

Now all I had to worry about was this revocation hearing. I knew Money was out there going crazy without his road dog and partner in crime. I couldn't wait until the day I'd be welcomed home again.

# Chapter 25

## *SIX HUNDRED*

I ain't never hurt a soul that I didn't have to. Every nigga that ever got it, I felt deserved that shit. Nah, I ain't God. Not even close. I'm only human. The only flame I've seemed to regret at times, is the blaze I sent my Pops. Then again, I truly believe shooting a nigga like him in the leg or some shit would have certainly resulted in my own death. My decision was rash, but it wasn't omissible. He had no right! Beating on my mama like she was some nigga off the streets. I miss him, though. I miss the shit outta dude. I miss my momma and my sister too. In killing him, I've also killed the relationship I had with them.

I still remember everything he taught me. One of his main quotes was, *"Whatever you decide to do in this life, be sure to do your best at it."* He taught me that there is no substitute for hard work.

Momz just let a nigga go. I kinda understand. But, at heart, I feel like she chose Tawanna over me. I can't really be mad at her about it. Though, I do find myself resenting her at times. I still love her to death, no doubt. We ain't close as we used to be but we talk every three to four months. Somehow, I ain't been home since. Sometimes I miss Chicago. After all, it's home. Tawanna just turned twelve, I've seen a few recent pictures of her. The few times they've came this way have been crazy. Momz' city still love a nigga, but the repugnancy I feel from Sis hurt! We used to be best friends.

Despite our age differences, she had always been my little angel. I wonder why she can't see that I was just protecting our mother. Momma say she just need a little time. It's been five muthafuckin' years! She was a daddy's little girl. Every time she sees me, she runs from me. I guess she sees me as some sort of monster. Laying here thinking about all that has happened in my seventeen years on this earth, I wonder where my life is heading. I mean, I wanna do good. But it seems like all these niggaz understand is violence.

So, if that's what they want, I'll gladly give it to 'em. Seeing myself stretched out, full of bullet holes and no vital signs is something I'll only see when I'm dead. It's said that we see it all when our spirits depart from these shells that we call bodies. That's some supernatural shit. I ain't ready to go! I gotta get 'em first! Either we gon' make the news, or you gon' make it. I'd rather it be you with the misfortune of being found slain. I'll take the fortune, cause that's what I'm in it for. You can have the spotlight when it comes to all that rah-rah shit.

I'm just a young nigga trying to live! You hear me? What better revenge is there than gettin' rich? If niggaz hating the lil money we gettin' now! This is just the epitome of how I'm gon' start eradicating niggaz. Check it. Me and Honesty ran into the nigga Mighty and a few of his people on a couple occasions. The clown—ass nigga thought shit was real funny.

Honesty had no idea who he was though. It was hard for me to keep my emotions in check. I wanted to catch him and Proof together, so I could hit 'em both at the same time. Since I ain't been seeing them together like I used to, I decided to make Mighty priority number one. I'm thinking, shit won't be so funny after today! I'm colder than a muthafucka! These weak ass gloves ain't doin' shit! They're too thin. We've been laying on this nigga for a week. Somehow, Doe found out he stayed out here on Layard Avenue. That's where we at now.

It's a relatively quiet neighborhood. From what we've seen the information is valid. Him, his bitch and their eight-year-old daughter stays here. We've seen Tamieko, her daughter and a few of her chicken-head ass fiends come and go. Mighty too, though he ain't here much. I just personally watched this hoe-nigga go up in there at about 2:00 a.m. this morning. I've been under this bitch's porch waiting ever since! So, I can light his ass up. Today's murder kit consisted of a black Gorilla mask and a snub nose .357 Mag. My patience was running low. If he didn't come outta there soon, I was kickin' the door in. I was hoping he'd came right back out, but he didn't.

Telesis was under the porch directly across the street from me. She was probably over there talkin' shit, and as cold as I was. This November weather ain't no joke! A nigga fuck around and catch the pneumonia. It was 7:33 a.m., he shoulda been on his way out to take his baby girl to school at any minute now. We've seen him on his route a few times. The door opened and I slowly crept from underneath the house, hoping I wasn't undetected. I ain't wanna do it like this. Shorty gon' hate apes forever after witnessing this shit. It is what it is, I pulled the hammer back on the Smith & Wesson in a crouching position on the side of the house.

# Chapter 26

## *DOE*

### *A Cold Summer*
### *Four Months Prior*

*"Fresh out of the paint shop, I slid down 3rd in Chambers in my four door Chevy Impala. I've got the gold specs in the light brown paint. The coffee-brown rag, gold buttons and chrome strips. The doomed front end, big boy grill and the triple gold Ds and Vogues made everybody on the block come to a standstill. Subbing, I've got six tens mounted across my back seat. I got my shit bangin' so hard as I hit the route, it sounds like King Kong and his momma in the trunk tryna' get out. The 6x9s and the tweeters merging with the bass growl, I'm welling that Eazy!"*

Nodding my head slowly as I sang along with the lyrics.

"Cause the Boyz N The Hood are always hard. Come talkin' that trash we'll pull ya card. Knowin' nothin' in life, but to be legit. Don't quote me boy, cause I ain't said shit—"

Pulling up in front of the spot, the young squadron were all smiles at my arrival. First off, you had the head and brains of the crew, Smoke. This lil' nigga happened to love books just as much as he loves the streets. Second in command was the big shorty Six. On everything, he was huge to be his age. At seventeen, lil' folks got twelve murders under his belt. Sadly, one of the bodies happened to be the death of his own father. After that, I guess he just didn't give a fuck. One day, he came home from school to find his father in the house beating his mother. This was something he'd witnessed on many occasions.

Though he loved them both, his mother is his heart. However, at age eleven he was no match for his father. One of whom stood six-foot-four and weighed close to three-hundred pounds.

***

Glancing over his father's shoulder, he saw her eye. It was swollen shut and had turned black and blue. Her mouth was bleeding as well. Her lips had swelled to the point where they no longer looked like they were hers. Her top lip was damn near touching her nose. His sister, Tawanna was only seven at the time. She had her knees pulled to her chest, balled in the corner of the living room, crying. Six went to break-up the slaughter, as his father continued to throw blows to his mother's body.

Grabbing his father from behind, he wrapped his frail arms around his father's waist as much as he could. "Get off my momma!" he yelled.

His father brushed him off with ease. He turned around and hit Six in his ear so hard, he'd almost lost consciousness as he fell. That night, right there before his family's eyes, the unthinkable occurred. Using a .38 Special he'd bought off the streets, Six shot his father in his face three times at pointblank range. When the authorities arrived, though distraught his mother covered for him the best she could. She told them gang members invaded their home, accusing her husband of selling drugs in their territory. That they'd beat her and her son in an attempt at retrieving the money they believed he'd had.

When he'd failed to provide them with neither cash nor drugs, he was executed. To this day, his sister fears him. It's to a degree where she stopped speaking to him all together. Anytime he's in her presence it seems to take her back to that night. She'll balled up somewhere and cry, rocking back and forth. She was so traumatized his mother decided to send him to Wisconsin to live with his auntie.

Then, you've got the two brothers of the crew, Freak and Brew. For whatever reason the ladies seem to love these two fools. Crook is the loudmouth and comedian of the squad. We call him Crook because he loves robbing shit. He's the unpredictable type. Then we've got Thirty. Wise beyond his years when it comes to certain aspects of the game, he tends to act shy around women. My lil' nigga a beast, though.

They're all straight shooters. Some would say there's good havoc amongst us if there is such a thing. I got out and showed everybody some love. It was time to open up shop. I saw Moo's green Chevy, so I knew he was already on deck. It was time to get this paper.

## Chapter 27

### *SIX*
### *We Ready*

Though it had only been a few weeks since J.L.'s death, the twins were letting us run wild. We were moving everything from crumbs to bricks. The connect kept us flooded and business was good. Doe preached the same sermon to us every day before opening up shop.

"Be careful," he'd say. "Never know who got their eyes on you and think you a lick." Our main two dope houses were on 3rd in Chambers.

Smoke, Brew and Thirty ran cocaine out of one spot while me, Freak, and Crook ran the Heroin out the other. At times we'd switch so the entire crew would know the math on both products. Moo and Doe oversaw the operation from a third location across the street. Nobody knew how we ran the operation outside our immediate circle. Today, it was Freak, Crook and Brew's turn to stand on security. Crook had the corner on 3rd in front of the paint shop. Brew was down the street in front of John's Red Hots.

Freak was around the corner on Burleigh, in Rose Park. It was August afternoon and the sun was just getting started. At ninety-eight degrees, the humidity made it feel like it was fifteen degrees hotter than it was. Needless to say, the block was secure. Crook hit the transmitter button on his walkie-talkie for the umpteenth time.

"Yo'! Freak, Brew!"

"What's up?" Freak was first to respond, then Brew.

"Yeah, what's up, nigga?"

"Man, it's hotter than wild wolf booty out here, ain't it!" There was static for a few seconds, then Brew responded to Crook's rhetoric.

"Yeah, it's hot! Damn, don't you think we know that? I'ma give yo' fat ass something hotter, nigga! Stay the fuck off the hummer unless you see some fuckin' money or the Jakes!" Brew snapped.

"Damn, Brew, is that your breath I'm smelling through this walkie-talkie, boy? You need to take care of that! Somebody please—please relieve him! Relieve him!" Crook joked. Then he said, "Nah, for real though. Benny K on his way around there. I just talked to him."

I chimed in, "I got 'em. I knew that nigga would be back."

Doe gave us a stiff warning, overhearing the conversation, "Six, you and Tank be on point. Don't forget Benny's old ass got a few tombstones under his belt. Don't get comfortable."

"He can come up here and see 3C on some bullshit if he wanted to," I replied, peering through the blinds. "We ready. M-16 ready."

"That's peace!" Thirty chimed in. As soon as Benny stepped foot on the porch, I greeted him. Swinging the door open, I said, "B.K., what's up, playa?"

"Shit, man, just trying to get this here monkey off my back," he replied, scratching his arms. "Six, let me get something for fifty real quick." He smiled showing me his infamous grin.

His whole top was gone, all I saw was his gums. I allowed him to step inside the kitchen and closed the door. Benny had no idea Tank was in the pantry pointing an assault rifle at him. I walked past him and headed for the counter to weigh his package. Giving him my back, I had faith that if the known killa made any sudden moves the big homie Tank would lay him down.

*I bet every time this nigga comes through here, he thinks a nigga is in here alone,* I thought.

Though we were responsible for moving the work, the twins also assigned a shift to each 3C member to post in both spots with something heavy, females included. I'm sure Benny had thought about hittin' us. He wasn't stupid, though. He knew how niggas got down. If he tried it, he'd never make it off the block. Seeing the communication was tight, he played it cool.

"Where Domain at?" he asked, reaching for the money to make the transaction.

"Oh, Doe? He's always around. Why? You need me to tell 'em something for you?" I asked.

"Nah, just tell him I came by." He eyed the pack, as if he could weigh it by just looking at it. "I've been knowing him and Moo since they were babies."

"Aw, believe me. They already know you're here," I replied.

He didn't even respond, I guess he didn't know how to. What I'd just told him had to have his head fucked up. He glanced around the kitchen. I bet he was wondering if we had cameras mounted. Or were we simply working with the walkie-talkies and the good set of binoculars he always saw sitting out in plain sight. We had the block sewed up. Benny pocketed his shit and got up outta there. Tank came out of the pantry sweating like he'd just ran a marathon.

I said, "Daaamn! I bet you almost murdered his ass when he reached for that money, huh?" Tank not being a man of many words, nodded in agreement. "Crazy muthafucka, you." I gave him some dap. "Yeah, that was a close one. But we good," I assured. "At ease soulja. Until the next one." I laughed, giving him a salute.

The day went smooth. We clocked over fifty thousand with ease. By nightfall, it was time to shut shit down as usual. For us, this meant it was time to kick it. We were outside in front of the spot trying to figure out where we were heading. Smoke was standing on the hood of the brand-new white Regal he and Thirty shared. Doe copped three Cutlass Oldsmobiles and two Buick Regals for the squad.

"So, what's up, niggaz? I got two for GDs." Smoke held up two fingers as *LL Cool J's I'm Bad* rattled the windows of the Cutty. "A nigga like me got plans though."

I said, "Shit, I'm trying to get me some for sure pussy. Y'all already know my—"

"Honestyyy's!" the rest of the camp said in unison.

Niggaz tryin' to bust me out before I even got a chance to finish the sentence. Honesty is my main thang. That's wifey. She stands about 5'6, petite and light-skinned. My baby's bad and there's always a gang of bad bitches at her crib. She's head of a group that call themselves Complete. They rep 3C as well. There is no denying it, complete they are. Young, fine and sexier than a muthafucka!

What originally started as three young ladies coming together to form a R&B group grew into some of the finest female crews the city has seen in a minute. There will always be the original three. Honesty, Telesis and Jillian. Then, Ushi and Scaifee joined the group. Not to mention the other eleven or so that roll with them, are just as bad.

I said, "Hell yeah Honesty's, niggaz! Don't y'all love the sound of that? I do." Wasn't no shame in my game. I was thinkin' about my better half.

Freak said, "He's got a point. It's always a slew of beautiful young ladies through that joint. They stay thick! I'm with you."

"Aw, nigga." Thirty folded his arms in protest. "You just saying that because you got some pussy over there before." He frowned.

"I think everybody out here got some pussy over there, but yo' ass!" Smoke butted in making fun of him.

"Fuck you, niggas!" Thirty spat.

He ain't like that shit, but Smoke was speaking the truth.

I said, "For real! You can't be freezing up every time you get around all that beauty. Closed mouths don't get fed, my nigga."

"I'm with Honesty's!" Brew yelled, as he flinched at Thirty. They squared up.

"Well, that's what's up," Smoke said, jumping off the car as Thirty and Brew went in circles slap boxing, he said, "I enjoy being surrounded by pussy like a maxi-pad."

Freak said, "Ugh, bloody ones, too."

We all laughed.

Smoke said, "Never, fool. Let me holla at Doe nem. Hold up." Hitting the key on his walkie-talkie, Doe responded right away.

"What's up?" Doe asked.

"Yo, this Smoke."

"I know, I'm lookin' at you."

"We about to be out. We're heading over by Honesty's crib."

"Y'all lockup and everything?" he asked.

"Yeah, Dynamite and Capone loose, too," he replied.

Capone is a German Shepherd that stands over six feet on his hind legs. He was so vicious, his eyes literally turned red when he's angry. Dynamite is a female tiger striped Pit. She's just as dangerous. After shop closed, we'd turn them loose. One in each spot, just in case a fiend or bum ass nigga wanna play cat burglar.

"Sounds like everything's good to me," Doe came back.

Moo chimed in, "We'll call you or slid though there if we need you."

"A'ight," he replied.

Moo said, "Peace, be safe."

"Peace, I'm out," Smoke replied. "Look, everybody go shower or whatever. Get dressed. We gon' meet up over by my crib. I don't know about y'all, but I'm wearing that shit we copped at the mall yesterday. It's seven thirty now. Try to make it to my house within an hour."

Everybody agreed, our Friday night had just begun.

# Chapter 28

## *Blackberry Molasses*

It was about 9:15 when we hit the block that cool summer night. Honesty's and a bar called Glory Daze down on Burleigh were our favorite places to kick it. The hood was always where we we're most comfortable. Honesty and her crew were on her porch thirteen deep. They were in a heated debate on who held the crown as the rawest female MC in the game? *Lyte, Salt, Pep, Roxanne Shante', or The Real Roxanne?* Honesty had just finished Kami's last French braid when we pulled up four cars deep. They always fucked with the squad when we came through. This night would be no different.

Honesty stood up and started shouting, "Oh! Oh-oh-ohhh!" She did The Whop.

Her entire crew followed her lead. They were happy to see us. The Hoodfellas. The Low End came to life as the ladies chanted and twisted their fingers, throwing up 3C. We got out and posted in front of the whips as if we were posing for pictures. We all wore Nikes and Adidas. We stood across the street and watched as Complete did their thing.

Honesty then calmed her girls, "Hold up, y'all! Hold up, Complete!" she told them, then greeted me, "What's up, Six? I see you all fresh and shit, nigga!" Mimicking us, she crossed her arms putting on a B-Boy stance of her own, she yelled, "Uh-ohhhh!"

Her crew echoed her taunt. All the ladies were now in B-Boy mode. I smiled.

"What's up, babe? What's all that shit y'all were just doing with y'all hands?"

She said, "You know what it is. That there be three-cee!" She threw it up again. "Three-Complete! You see it? Fuck Chambers, nigga!"

I tapped Smoke. "Dog, you seeing and hearing this shit?"

He said, "Hell yeah. And we ain't havin' it. Get 'em!"

Running across the street toward the ladies, Complete members scattered laughing and screaming. The tables quickly turned for us.

We were outnumbered, and a few of us were getting jumped. Though Honesty tried to flee, I caught up to her down the street trying to hide behind a tree.

"Wait! Waait! Hold up!" She laughed, backing up. "Don't! You bet not hit me, Six!"

"Oh, now it's wait? How you gon' holler fuck the block then talk about wait? Where your gangsta at?" I moved in closer.

"Help! Heelp!" Freak came flying past us with three Complete members on his ass.

Honesty yelled, "Complete! Oho!"

Meka and Diamond noticed that I had their girl cornered and came to her aid and assist. Fia continued to run Freak down.

"Here go my gangsta, right here! Nigga, what!" Honesty got bold, seeing her girls grab me from behind.

Meka was on my back, and Diamond was trying her best to pull me to the ground by dragging her body low.

"What you trying to do to my girl, nigga!" Meka yelled, choking me playfully as I maneuvered in position to overpower them.

"Uh-uh! Where you going?" Diamond said, wrapping her frame around my legs. She held on to me with all her might.

"Wait, hold up!" I yelled, holding on to my pants.

I was trying to keep my gun from falling down the pants leg of my Adidas jumpsuit. Honesty saw me trying to clutch and snatched my pistol from my waistband.

She said, "Oooh! Look what I got!" She tucked it in the back of her shorts. "And I know you didn't just holler wait? I gotcha gun. Now look at you. You so weak. Poor, baby. Where yo' gangsta at, huh?" She smiled, then she pushed me.

I lost my balance and fell; I couldn't believe I'd allowed them to get me on the ground.

"A'ight, y'all. I got 'em from here," she called her girls off. "Don't move, nigga! Stay down! If you move, I'ma pop you," she warned me hand behind her back clutching my gun.

"Oh, so that's how you gon' do me, huh?" I asked, throwing my hands up in submission.

"Yup!" She mean-mugged me.

"That's how you gon' do meee!" I yelled, springing to my feet. Scooping her up over my shoulder.

I carried her back down the block.

"Boy, put me down! Put me down, Six!" she screamed and squirmed.

"Be still, girl." I held her tight, snatching my gun from the back of her Duke's. "Gimme this damn gun. What chu doin' with this?" I tucked it back in its place.

It was a beautiful night out. Everybody was out there running around having fun. Even Thirty had joined in on the squabble, which was uncharacteristic of him. He had Demetria hemmed up against one of the Regals. What he didn't see, was Pookie and Yahma creeping up behind him.

"Nigguh, what! What, nigguh! Huh!" they yelled, as they grabbed him and flung him to the ground.

"Oh, shit!" Thirty yelled, laughing.

I just smiled as I continued to glance around. I saw Smoke and Crook had their hands full. I searched the block looking for Freak and Brew.

*Where my niggaz at?* I thought.

Honesty was still squealing and kicking away. Movement between her crib and the house next door caught my attention. I looked a little closer to find Brew and Freak. Their hands were roaming and groping the bodies of Ushi and Nichole as if they hadn't seen each other in years.

*Look at these niggas,* I thought. *And these fools acting like they didn't wanna come over here.*

I carried Honesty up on her porch and put her down.

# Chapter 29

## *Rock Witcha*

"Now that I've got you all to myself." I rubbed my hands together, staring at her seductively. "Anybody in the house?" I moved in closer and grabbed her by her waist.

"Why?" she asked, wrapping her arms around my neck as she stared into my eyes.

"Cause." I smooched her lips. "I wanna go—" I smooched those soft lips again. "In the house." I kissed her neck. "And turn off the lights," I whispered in her ear, then kissed it. "Lock all the doors, and—"

"Shhh." She put her index finger to my lips. "You can show me the rest. Hold up." She smiled. "Ushi! Scaifee!" she called out to her homegirls, but there was no response. She smacked her lips and threw her hand on her hip. "Now I know y'all hear me! Scaifee!" she called out again.

"Ooh, shit! What's up, Hon?" Scaifee answered in her sweet, sexy tone, sounding out of breath.

"Damn! I know y'all ain't on the side of my house fuckin'? That's just nasty!"

"Nall, girl!" she answered with the quickness.

Ushi said, "Now you know, shawty! Uh-uh!" she had much attitude in that Georgia drawl of hers.

Honesty said, "What I do know is niggaz had y'all asses tongue tied. I'm about to go in the house for a minute!"

"What? A minute?" I whispered, sucking on her neck.

She said, "Shut up, boy. I'm locking this door! If Telesis come through—"

"We got it!" Ushi replied.

"Come on." She took me by my hand, leading me through her home, straight to her bedroom.

I flopped down on the bed, laid back and threw my arms behind my head relaxing. I couldn't help but admire that model posture in her frame as she walked over to the stereo. She opened the glass door and bent all the way over to grabbed some tapes from the bottom of the entertainment system.

*Ooh, shit!* I thought.

My dick was getting hard already. I was trying to stay calm, but the Daisy Dukes were fitting her oh, so well. She was showing me a lil' bit of them ass cheeks, and a lot of legs. Her shorts seemed as if they were painted on. She stood up, shuffling through the cassettes she had in her hands. Selecting one, she put it in, and pressed play.

I damn near jumped out my skin when the *Isley Brothers* blasted through her sub-woofers. *I'm yo' brother/ I'm yo' brotha/Don't cha know/I'm yo' brothaaaah!*

"Damn, bae, turn that shit down!" I plugged my ears.

Apparently, she was a little stunned as well. She hadn't realized she'd left the stereo's volume on full blast when she and Complete were listening to it from the porch earlier. She quickly adjusted the knob, turning it down.

"Oops! My bad." She giggled.

"Yeah, I know. And what the hell? I am *not* your brother."

"Six, you don't know about the Isley's?" She sucked her teeth. "Yo' young ass."

"Baby, my momma know about the Isley's." I hopped off the bed. "Give 'em here. Let me see the tapes." I held my hands out.

"Okay, fine with me. You pick somethin' then. Everything else is under there, too. I gotta use the bathroom anyway." She pouted, stomping toward her bedroom door.

"A'ight, now. And, hey!" I stopped her in her tracks.

"What, Marcus?" She turned around.

"And wash yo' damn hands, too." I chuckled.

"I know! Boy please, you is not my daddy." She smiled, switchin' hard as she could as she left the room.

*Okay,* I thought, selecting two tapes that piqued my interest.

I put both in and adjusted the volume a little bit. I pressed play on deck one. It wasn't quite where I wanted it, so I pressed fast forward for a second. Checking it again, I found the song I was looking for. It was ready. I pushed play on deck two, rewinding some, then another brief check. It was in the middle of the song I was looking for. I pressed rewind for a few more seconds and pushed play.

The silence told me it was ready as well. Looking around the room, I took my gun from my waistband and placed it in the drawer next to the bed. As soon as Honesty walked back in, I pushed play on tape deck one. *Barry White's* baritone voice came bursting through the speakers. I was giving my best impression of the icon as I lip sang his classical hit, *Never, Never Going To Give You Up.*

I was putting on my best tango, too. "Six, what are you doing?" Honesty asked as she stood in the doorway laughing while I put on my show.

I pushed pause. "Okay, bae, wait. All jokes aside. You can turn the lights down but stay right there. Let me come get you." I pushed play on tape deck two, walked over to her and scooped her up in my arms. "Listen," I whispered in her ear as I laid her on the bed and removed her sandals.

The melodies of *Bobby Brown's Rock Witcha* played. She adjusted her body, welcoming me as Bobby began to serenade.

*Now that you are here with me/Baby let's do it right/Lady you know just what I need/I want to hold you, oh so tight—*

I unbuckled her belt and unbuttoned her shorts. Caressing her body, I laid beside her and began tongue kissing her as I unzipped her shorts. She gave me all access to her body, stretching her arms above her head as she laid flat on her back. Using my tongue, I gyrated from her lips to her neck, shoulders, and her perfect sized erect nipples.

"Ooh, Six, you got me wet. Take it all off me," she moaned as her body began to shake. I stood up and slid her shorts and her panties off together. "Take that shit off and come get this pussy," she moaned in a sexy voice, that I wanted to hear again as I undressed her.

"What you say?"

"Come get it, nigguh," she purred, staring in my eyes.

She licked her lips and rubbed her clit. Shit, I wasted no time removing my clothes, sliding on protection and catering to her needs.

"Sssss! Awwww!" She braced herself grabbing my ears in excitement.

I slid her to the edge of the bed so that pussy was right in my face. I licked and sucked her sweet peach. My taste buds relishing her mellifluous nectar as her juices began to flow. It got so good to her, as she creamed, she began begging me to get inside her.

"Get in the bed with me. Give it to me! I need it right now. Fuck me!" She pulled me on top of her and arched her back as I entered her missionary style. "Babyyy, ooooh!" she moaned.

I went deep and paused for a second as I tongued her down. The moisture and softness of lips brought my erection to its full potential. I grabbed a handful of her hair and gently pulled it as I began exploring her walls. I sucked on her neck using my lips and my tongue at the same time for suction. The spark and levin I'd always felt when our bodies collide, is like nothing I've never felt before. It's always the maximal pleasure. I slid my hands underneath her ass, positioning her pussy at an upward angle as I put my back in every stroke, going deeper and deeper.

"Ahh! Ahhhh! Aww shit, Six, don't stop," she moaned as I rolled my hips making sure she felt every inch.

"Ooooh! Oooh! Ooooh! Sssss!" she cried, throwing it back at me.

She rolled over on top of me. I started throwing it up at her.

"Aww! Ummmm, shit! I love this dick!" she screamed.

"All you love is this dick, huh!" I taunted and stroked even harder with each word.

"I-I love you! I love you! Get it! Get this pussy!" She pounced up and down and rolled it.

Palming her ass cheeks with both hands, I sped up the pace. Our bodies clapped in harmony.

"Awww! Awwww, shit!" she cried passionately.

*Boom! Boom! Boom! Boom! Boom!*

*What the fuck?* I thought as I grabbed Honesty and rolled over onto the floor as slugs whizzed through the walls.

"Honesty, stay down! Somebody shootin' at the house! Stay down!" I yelled.

I crawled toward the other side of the bed. Reaching in the drawer, I grabbed my gun as shots continued to ring outside.

*Bo! Bo! Bo! Bo! Bo! Bo! Bo!*

"Fuuuuck," I seethed, unable to move.

There was the sounds of screeching tires. Suddenly, relief. Then a few seconds of silence.

"Aaaah! Aaaah!" I heard a female scream.

"N-o-o-o-o! Nooo! Oh my God! Noooo!" Another female yelled.

"Aw nall! Hell nall, shawty!"

Different screams and groans could be heard from the Complete crew. Honesty's bedroom window was right there on the front porch.

"Nooooo! Nooo! Help us! Somebody help us! She's hit! She's hit! Autumn! Autumn, breathe, just breathe!" I heard another female yell.

Jumping to my feet, gun in hand I tried to get my pants on as fast as I could.

"What the fuck you doing? Don't move her! Gotdamit!" I heard Freak's voice. He started banging on the window.

"Honesty, call an ambulance! I'm goin' outside!" *Look at this shit,* I thought. There were three big ass holes in Honesty's bedroom wall. "Honesty!" I called out again, but I got no response. Walking over to the side of the bed where I'd left her, I dropped my gun and fell to my knees. She'd been hit. "Aw nall, Hon." I gently lifted her head and laid it in my lap. Grabbing the phone cord, I drug the phone to me.

"911 Operator. What's your emergency?" the lady on the other end asked.

"We need help! There's been a shooting at 1024 Locust. My baby's hit." I let the phone fall to the floor, as tears fell from my eyes.

# Chapter 30

## *PROOF*
## *Thuggin'*

On the North side, me and Mighty were just making a left on Burleigh. The drive-by we'd just pulled happened on some drunk humbug shit. We'd came to the conclusion that we were no longer in agreement with the bullshit *peace* talk that Zoo put in everybody's ear. We were sitting at the bar inside People's getting drunk. Reminiscing on all the niggaz we'd lost, we decided to head East and see who we could catch slippin'. When we hit 3rd in Locust and spotted the two Oldsmobiles and the two Buicks, we had our targets.

Noticing a lot of movement on the block, Mighty told me to pull over so we could peep the scene for a minute. We were in a Chevy Mighty had recently purchased, so we went unnoticed. I tried to reason with him once I saw all the females out there. But he didn't give a fuck. He gave me an ultimatum.

He told me, "Nigga, you can get up out this muthafucka and take your chances walking back to the block or get to bussin' your gun!"

Going against my better judgment, I decided it was time to ride. We took off our shirts, tied them around our faces, and cocked our weapons. Mighty had a 7-Ball, I had a .410 sawed off shotgun. We pulled up to the spot, knowing more than likely, there were a lot niggaz inside. Our plan was to act normal, as if nothing happened. When we walked in, we were greeted by U-Tee, Brando, Who-Man, Kane and eleven-year-old Wink. Trying to be just like us, Wink was always trying to kick it like he was grown.

It was after midnight, and Wink's lil' ass should've been at home somewhere, but here he is. They had a game of Spades going. All that could be heard besides Big Daddy Kane playing in the background, was, "Lawd! Lawd! What's up, Lord!"

Knowing they were all Gangstaz, they loved fuckin' with us. Some called it Bogus Bangin' when you had oppositions coming together as one. Who gives a fuck about right or left? When the only color that really matters is green. We shook up with our niggaz.

U-Tee said, "Where y'all niggaz disappear to? We was lookin' for y'all. I know the bar was dead, but damn."

"Where y'all go, Lawd? To get some pussy?" Wink asked with a smile.

Mighty laughed. "What yo' lil' ass know about some pussy nigga? Nothing! But, nah, we ain't go hit nothin'. I had a few moves I needed to make. I asked my nigga to ride with me. After that, we just hit a few blocks."

Kane looked at me sideways, but he ain't say shit. He just continued to smoke and sip his Old English. He secretly envied me, cause I was fuckin' his ex-bitch. He acted so nonchalant about it, I thought he didn't give a fuck.

"What you niggaz been up in here doing?" Mighty questioned.

Brando said, "Shit! Drinking, smokin' weed and catching money. Ain't shit been happening."

Mighty said, "I hope y'all ain't let Wink little knucklehead ass hit none of that shit. Boy, where yo' momma? She gon' beat that ass, and you know it!" He grabbed Wink and put him in a headlock.

"Shit, I'm grown," Wink said, pushing Mighty off him.

Mighty said, "Aw, you grown, huh? Well, why yo' lil' ass always runnin' when Tre-Foe Pam pull on the block then, huh?" Wink just looked at him wearing half a smile.

"Cause you know you and whoever she catches you with gettin' that ass beat, too, right?"

"Oooh, yeah I know," Mighty taunted.

We all laughed. Wink couldn't deny that shit, so he laughed with us.

After the laughter settled, Mighty asked Kane, "How much money been coming through?"

He said, "Man, shit been slow. I mean, extra slow. It seems like all the fiends done vanished since that beef with the other side and J.L. got hit."

U-Tee said, "You right. Money has been slow as fuck. I wonder why that is?"

"Damn, I thought I was trippin'." I scratched my head. "I know Zoo noticed this shit. I wonder why he ain't said nothing?"

"I wouldn't worry about it. I'm sure he'll address it," U-Tee said, taking a swig of his half pint of Remy.

"Come on, Wink. I'm taking yo' lil' ass home," Mighty announced, grabbing his keys.

# Chapter 31

## *MOO*
## *Pandemonium*

St. Joseph's was surrounded when we pulled up. Although the police tried to contain the traffic, cars were still arriving by the minute. The main waiting area was packed. Everybody was crying with tears pouring down their faces. The sadness unequivocally clear. Honesty's fifteen-year-old cousin was DOA, and Honesty was in critical condition. She'd took a slug to the chest. Autumn's mother had dropped her off at Honesty's just minutes before the shooting occurred. Honesty had no idea her cuz was even outside. When Honesty's mother and uncle rushed through the emergency room doors, it was obvious they'd already heard.

Debra came at Six like a lioness. "Six, what happened!" She threw blows at his face and chest. Due to her hysteria, they were weak. He easily dodged those aimed at his face, allowing the chest shots to connect before grabbing her. "What chu do! What chu doooo! What did you do, Marcuuuus!" she cried.

Her clamor caused other members of Complete to cry out as well. Six remained silent. I could tell her words were soul crushing, but he held her tight.

"Why they shoot my baby's house up like that? Who did it? Who hurt my ba-baby?" she wailed.

Autumn's mother, Sherry had just arrived. She came through the doors frantically screaming her daughter's name.

"Autumn! Autuuumn!" She searched the faces of all the young ladies present, their heads dropped. "Deb, where— where's Autumn?" she asked, confused of not seeing her among the others.

Debra was befuddled, she hadn't heard anything about Autumn being out there. She searched Six's eyes, he shook his head. "Autumn wa-was?" Debra questioned him.

He said, "She ain't make it. She-she got hit, too. She ain't make it, Ma!"

Debra gasped for breath. "N'awwww! Awwww! Aw, Autumn!" Sherry broke down as well.

Honesty's uncle Fabe caught Sherry as she dropped to her knees. It sounded like a funeral, right there in the hospital.

"Get off me! I gotta see 'em! Get off of me!" Debra yelled.

"Let her go, nigga!" Honesty's uncle roared while holding Sherry in his arms.

Six mugged him because of his tone. This wasn't the time or place for egotistic behavior. He let it slide. He eased up on his hold on Debra. As soon as he released her arms, she smacked the shit out of him. He was stunned, but mostly hurt by her actions. She'd always loved him and treated him like a son. We were all feeling her pain. He didn't say or do anything. He simply dropped his head in shame.

Sniffling, he wiped his tears. "Honesty's gon' make it. I know she will." Walking over to Sherry and Fabe, he said, "I'm sorry about Autumn."

He looked at me and Doe, then nodded toward the exit. Young 3C followed his lead. Doe told Telisis and a few more soldiers to keep an eye on the shorties.

As they were leaving, Debra yelled, "That's right! Getcha ass up outta here and go find whoever did this shit, nigga! Marcuuus! Marcus, you hear meee! Find them mutha-fuckaaaaz!" I'm sure he heard her loud and clear, and planned on doing just that.

As 3C left the hospital, they were being watched. They were being photographed along with everybody that came and left, by none other than the FBI. As they'd made their way through the crowd of spectators outside, questions came from every direction. All the inquiries fell upon deaf ears. I knew from that look he gave us, Six had murder on his mind and nothing short of it would satisfy him. He was moving so fast, he'd gotten ahead of the crew.

Brew called out to him, then jogged up, catching by the whip. "Aye, yo' slow up. Where you goin'? You know we down for whatever, right?"

Seeing the blank stare in his homie's eyes, he knew what was up.

"Follow us to my crib real quick. Then, we goin' to kill somethin'. Smoke, come on, nigga!" Six yelled, before jumping in the car.

He slammed the door and started it up.

When Smoke made it to the passenger side, he asked Brew, "What's up? What he say?"

"He said follow y'all," Brew replied, walking toward the Cutty.

Smoke yelled, "Freak, Crook! Everybody follow us!"

# Chapter 32

## *SIX*
## *Usual Suspects*

We gathered at my crib on $36^{th}$ in Clark. We were deep, but I wanted to speak directly to those who were at Honesty's when everything went down.

"A'ight, my niggas. Me and Smoke chopped it up on our way here. He ain't have no answers for me. I need somebody to fill me in on what the fuck happened out there."

Brew said, "On everything, all I know is I heard shots. But, by the time I got to the front all I saw was a grayish looking Chevy heading up the block. My niggas was dumpin' at it, so I start bussin', too!"

"What y'all see? Ain't nobody see no faces?" I questioned.

Crook took a deep breath and let out a sigh.

He said, "Man, shit happened so fast. But this what happen. It was me, Fia, Smoke, Diamond, and Shavon. At first, we were across the street by the cars listening to music. But, when Autumn and her momma pulled up, we put the weed out, got the drinks and came over to let shorty know you and Honesty were in the house with all the doors locked. That's when we sat on the porch.

"Thirty was in the cut talkin' to Donya. Freak and Brew were on the other side of the house fuckin' with Ushi and Nichole. Everybody else had already left. We was kickin' it. I was watching everything! Well, I thought I was. Then, this gray Chevy I'd never seen before pulled up.

"They had their shirts tied around their faces. The driver had the front passenger side window rolled down, shootin' through it. The other nigga came outta the driver's side back window over the roof. One high yellow nigga, and a black ass dude. Though their faces were covered, their upper bodies were fully exposed. It was—"

"Proof and Mighty?" I interrupted.

Crook said, "Yeah. Though they tried to hide it, it was them niggaz. We done shot it out with them fools so many times, I'd know them anywhere."

"How many of y'all bust y'all guns?" I looked around. "I know ain't neither one of 'em get hit. They would've come through the emergency room."

Thirty said, "Me, Crook, Smoke and Brew from what I saw. Smoke tried to pull everybody down and take cover. But damn." He shook his head. "Autumn."

"As fucked up as it is, we can't undo what's already done. You'll have a chance to redeem yourselves. Freak, what happened? Why you ain't buss?" I asked.

Salty at himself, he dropped his head. "Ain't no excuses on my part, G. I was slippin'. I left my heat in the car. But never again! Shorty, down, never again, my niggas! I promise you." He stacked 'em tall.

Smoke had already paged the twins. Twenty minutes went by, and I was beginning to grow impatient. Smoke decided he'd break the tension in the air.

He said, "Fuck it, we ain't gotta wait on 'em. That's why I got the key to the stash spot. For situations just like this. Let's go over to the spot, triple load and ride on them niggaz. They wanted us! So, let's ride for Complete. I know they're hurting right now. Let's ride for Honesty, Autumn and our muthafuckin' selves!"

Telesis said, "On 3C I'm goin'!" She was already blacked out, from the chin down. She said, "I say we take three cars! We split up. Any of them niggaz outside, whether they had something to do with it or not! It's lights out!"

Wintress said, "Let's ride down!"

The phone rung, Smoke answered it, "Hello? Yeah, what up, my nig?" Briefly covering the phone with his palm, he said, "Aye y'all, this Doe 'nem right here. Yeah, un-huh. Just give us the green light. You already know. He's right here. You wanna holla at 'em?" He looked at me. "Six, phone my dude."

I slowly walked over and grabbed the phone. In searching Smokes eyes for an inclination on what I was about to hear, I got nothing. I raised the phone to my ear. "Yeah, what up?" I paused. "The hospital? Y'all still there? For sure. I appreciate it, big bruh. Who, the doctor? They flying her to Freodert, right now?"

"What they say?" Telesis asked, seeing my facial expression harden.

I didn't wanna let that shit come off my tongue. It wasn't looking good. "She gon' make it! That's baby! I don't give a fuck what they talkin' about!" I handed the phone back to Smoke.

He said a few words, then hung up and said, "Fuck peace! Green light, niggas."

# Chapter 33

## *MIGHTY*

When we got outside, Wink noticed something right away that me or Proof hadn't. "Damn, Mighty! What happen to the Chevy thang, nigga!" Wink questioned.

"What you talkin' about?" I asked, walking over to the passenger side to see what he was referring to. I was still tipsy, and I staggered a lil' bit.

"Look!" He pointed. "Oooh! Them, bullet' holes ain't they?" Wink was excited.

"Shit!" I was thinking out loud. "Look, Wink," I said, "Don't say shit to nobody about this. You hear me?" He nodded. "Go in the house and tell Tee I said send me his keys."

"A'ight." Wink shrugged and started walking back in the spot.

"Nah, hold up." I stopped him. "Better yet, tell him I'm gon' need him to take you home. I gotta run somewhere real quick."

"Okay," Wink replied, before running back inside.

*How the fuck did I miss this shit!* I thought.

There were five bullet holes, two in the front door. One in the front quarter panel, and one had grazed the roof. I then counted another hole in the trunk. There was no telling who'd seen this shit.

I shook my head, jumped in and pulled off. *Damn nigga! You weren't thinkin'!* I pounded my skull. I had to at least attempt to hide the car before people started connecting me to the carnage and mayhem that transpired on the Eastside. There would be hell to pay if Zoo found out we'd been over there without his consent. I knew somebody out there had to get hit. I just didn't know who, I was trying to make it to my auntie's crib as fast as I could. Paying no attention to the speedometer, I hit Martin Luther King Drive doing sixty in a thirty-five mile per hour zone. I should've slowed the fuck down.

Before I knew it, all I heard were sirens blaring. I was being pulled over.

# Chapter 34

## *SIX*
## *Strapped*

When we hit Burleigh Zoo territory, we split up in threes. Me, Freak and Thirty hit 26th through 32nd. Smoke, Crook and Brew rode through 31st through 36th. There wasn't a soul in sight on our end we slid through. Smoke hit us on the walkie talkie. They said they hadn't run across anybody either. The police was thick. So, I told everybody to bring it in. Everybody responded accordingly besides one car.

Telesis said, "Hold on, Six. Not just yet." We'd made it back East, and it shocked us when we hit M.L.K. cause it was lit up!

I said, "Whoa! Oh, shit, Freak there go them people."

He said, "Just be cool. They sweatin' somethin'."

As we got closer, we saw five squads had somebody hemmed up. There were pedestrians young and old standing outside their homes being nosey.

I said, "Damn, they got the hood and the trunk up along with all the doors open on that muthafucka!"

Thirty said, "Slo—slow down, Freak. That look like a—"

"Grey Chevy," I finished his sentence.

When we rode past the officers were conducting the search and low and behold, standing at the back of the car's bumper in cuffs talking to one of the officers, was none other than Mighty. He glanced up at us as we cruised by at a slow pace in the Regal. We made eye contact. He knew we meant business. I'm pretty sure his heart started beating when he overheard the dispatcher radio in multiple gun shots being fired on 38th in Burleigh and asking all units to respond.

Meanwhile, Bella, Wintress, Telesis and Yetta were putting the finishing touches on a morning's work. "Bitch ass niggaz!"

Bella let the AK ride.

*Flocka! Flocka! Flocka! Laka! Laka! Laka! Laka!*

Telesis let the M-16 go as Yetta peeled out.

*Fac! Fac! Fac! Fac!*

They'd laid niggas down and stabbed out.

Bella yelled, "Yetta, slow this muthafucka down! Just be easy! All we gotta do is make it home. Do the speed limit."

Black and white cruisers shot past them sirens and lights flashing towards the scene.

Wintress said, "Don't look back. If they had a description of the car, they would've been busted a yewy. We good."

"I wonder, why they ain't have nobody on security, knowing they'd just came East shootin' shit up?" Bella questioned.

"Ha—haaa!" Wintress laughed. "Fuck 'em, they dead now. If they ain't, they'll be missing some chunks."

Telesis rode in silence, clutching the 16. No police in sight, Yetta relaxed. She turned the music up. A nigga from Oakland, named Too $hort was rappin' about money, hoes, cars and clothes.

# Chapter 35

## *SIX*
## *A Heavy Heart*

Although I'd sent hundreds of balloons, and twelve dozen roses ahead of me, I was still shook. All I knew was I had to see her. Walking in the hospital that day was bittersweet for me. It was one of the happiest, yet saddest days of my life. I didn't know what to expect. Would she blame me like her mother? The joy I felt knowing she'd made it, couldn't be described in words. Knowing the slugs weren't directed at her or Autumn weighed heavily on my heart. I tried to stay optimistic. I had to, I loved Honesty.

Debra, Telesis, Alisha, Kami, Ushi, Nichole and Jillian were all there when I walked in. I noticed the cold stare her mom gave me, as she was the first to face me. My eyes veered past her to my baby. She was still hooked up to an IV and a heart monitor as she laid staring out the window. Balloons and flowers filled the small room. The sudden quietness caught her attention, and she slowly turned her head to see me. I stood there in the doorway with a huge teddy bear and a paper bag in hand.

She smiled.

I spoke, "Hey-hey! Hey! Hey everybody."

"Hell nall, nigga. You—" Her mother went to stand.

Honesty grabbed her arm. "Ma, let me see him. I can't blame him for this. It's okay, give us a minute," Honesty's voice was faint.

It fucked me up seeing her in this condition.

"You sure?" Debra asked.

"Mm-hm." Honesty smiled, patting her mother's hand. "I'm sure."

"A'ight." She rolled her eyes. "But we ain't going nowhere, you hear? Come on, y'all." Debra stood.

Complete members got up as well. As they left, they all greeted me with hugs. Her mother was still mad at me. She kept it moving. I walked over to the table and sat the bag and the teddy bear down.

I walked over to her. "How you feelin'? I wish I could hug you, but I see they got you all bandaged up." I kissed her forehead, both cheeks, then her lips. "I'm so happy to see you." I caressed her face.

"Yeah, I'm okay. I'm happy to see you, too. Thank you for the cards and everything. The flowers are beautiful."

"Anything for my Tenderoni." I ran my fingers through her hair and said, "I'm sorry about cuz. That was my lil' homegirl."

"Yeah, Autumn was my sweetheart. The sister I never had that shared the same blood as me. I-I'm gonna miss her!" her voice cracked as she began to cry.

I wiped her tears away. "Shhhh. Come on, bae. Don't do that. Don't cry. You've gotta be strong so you can get up outta here."

"But she was coming to see me, Six!" she cried.

"I know! I know," I said, attempting to dry her tears. "But don't do that. I was coming to see you, too. I'd rather you blame me before I let you blame yourself." I had to do something to cheer her up somehow. "Look, I brought you your favorite ice cream. But you can't have any unless you're a big girl and stop all that cryin'. Come on." I looked into her eyes. "And guess what?" I grabbed the teddy bear. "Mr. Bear, got something to tell you." I went into my Cookie Monster impression. "I bought the chocolate chip cookies. I hear you luuuv some chocolate chip cookies!" I said playing the voice of the bear. "You gotta stop cryin'."

"Mmm-hmm." She wiped her tears away. "I'ma big girl, I want some ice cream."

"That's my girl. I knew you would. Let me get it for you." I handed her the teddy bear, then walked over and opened the bag. "Let's see what we got. I've got a bowl. A spoon, and your favorite, butter pecan ice cream. Oh, yeah, plus the cookies Mr. Bear bought with my money."

She giggled.

I was trying. "Get ready, I'm about to hook you up." I grabbed the ice cream and scooped out a bowl full, then grabbed the cookies. "You want these crushed up on top of this like you always eat it?"

"Yes, please." She pressed the button on the remote to move the bed so she could sit up.

"Damn, hold on. Let me stack your pillows behind you, baby." I rushed over, making sure she was comfy. "You a'ight?" I asked.

"Yes."

"You ready? I'm about to feed you."

"Yup, I'm ready," Honesty replied.

I took the bag of cookies, crushed them and sprinkled some on top of her ice cream, grabbing the bowl, then scooped some up on the spoon. "A'ight, open up, baby."

Honesty took in a mouthful. "Mmmm, this is good," she said, savoring her favorite desert.

"What they feed you this morning? Ain't nobody bring you nothin' to eat?"

"Mm-mmm!" She shook her head, holding up one finger as she chewed and swallowed. "Nope, I had to eat this nasty hospital food. Breakfast wasn't all that bad. I ordered a cheeseburger and some fries for lunch. Ain't nothing like some Mickey D's, though."

I said, "All you had to do was let somebody know you wanted some McDonald's. I would've made sure you got it."

She said, "Where yo' gees at? They ain't wanna see me?"

"They in the buildin'. Smoke and Brew in the waiting area. Freak covering the Emergency Room entrance and Tank in the lobby. I came up by myself for a reason. But believe me, they're anxious to see you. They love you, girl."

"They do, huh? And what about you?" she asked with a smile.

"Now you know I love me some Honesty, don't cha?" I smooched her lips.

"Yeah, I'm just sayin' though." She laughed.

"You just sayin' what?" I turned my back to her with the bowl.

"I'm just playin', boi. You bet not eat my ice cream." She reached for me, but I was too far away for her to grasp me.

I took a scoop anyway. "Damn, this is good."

I smiled.

She said, "Baby, can I ask you something?"

"Of course, anything, bae. Go 'head."

"Well—" She fiddled nervously with her fingers. I heard—"

"You heard what?" I licked the spoon.

"I heard five dudes got killed out on Burleigh last night. Was that y'all?"

"Here, your ice cream's melting, baby. Come on." I held up another spoon full.

She opened up and took it in, but I could tell she was still waiting on an answer.

I said, "Listen, Honesty, I know who shot y'all."

Her Heart rate on the EKG machine increased rapidly. "Ummmm!" She swallowed. "Who?" she questioned.

"Shhhh, calm down, I don't want you worrying about it. Just know I'm gon' make them niggas suffer. Them and anybody else in the way gon' catch flames. The less you know, the better. You know I can't tell you everything when it comes to the streets."

"Alright." She nodded.

"Knock! Knock!" Her mother stuck her head in the door. "Excuse me, Marcus. Do you mind if I come back in here with my baby, now? You know, I almost lost her," Debra said, misty eyed.

"Yeah, I know. We almost lost her. Get on in here, Ms. Brown. I wouldn't keep you from her. I was just feeding her some ice cream. That's all."

She came back in and announced that the girls had gone home to shower and change. They would be back later.

She told Honesty, "I'm gon' see what the doctor says. Hopefully, you can be discharged soon. I don't like hospitals. It's cold in here.

I whispered in Honesty's ear, "I'm gon' take care of everything. Here, open up."

# Chapter 36

## *U-TEE*

I was trying to figure out what the fuck was goin' on! Money being slow was one thing. Wales being killed was another. Now, I get a call at 3:00 a.m. concerning my nephews Wolfy, Lobo, and three of their friends being murdered on Burleigh. Nephew 'nem begged me to put them on. Now I'm regretting I'd done so. I knew that's where they made their money. What I'm trying to make some sense of, is why they were posted outside? They were beyond the block hustle. I made sure of that.

On second thought, maybe they'd just left the bar and went over there to check on shit. Had they gotten into it with somebody? Was it gang related? Was it a setup, or an attempt robbery or what?

A million thoughts raced through my mind. I'm stressin'. I'd made several phone calls, but don't nobody know shit. What puzzled me even more was that I hadn't heard from Mighty or Proof after several attempts to reach 'em. I'd been paging them ever since I got word of the killings but got no response. It wasn't like them at all. Zoo said he'd been trying to get at them as well.

It was now two in the afternoon, time for me to get out and about to see what's going on for myself. I had to go see my sister, then take a trip to the hood. I knew I'd never hear the end of this when it comes to Special.

I kept hearing her voice echo in my head, *"Tee, don't give my babies no dope."*

She'd been blowing my line up all morning. I was trying to avoid the inevitable. I was bound to receive a tongue lashing and more. Seeing her face to face would be different. Maybe she'd see that I'm also hurt by this and take it easy on me. That's what I was hoping for. Anyway, my phone rang. This time when my girl Sharon answered it, it was Congo. She handed me the phone.

"What's up? You still ain't heard from them brothaz?" I asked.

"Nope. Everybody I've spoken to says they ain't seen lil' buddy 'nem since People's."

"People's? When last night?"

"Yup?"

"Around what time?"

"Around seven-ish."

"I already know. I was there with 'em. They came to the spot a few hours later. You holla at Spree?"

"You know it. He said he ain't heard nothin'."

"Bullshit! All these muthafuckaz talking about they don't know nothin'!"

"Something ain't right, my nigga. First Wales, and now the lil' homies get sprayed up. What's up with Sis?"

"I'm on my way out there right now."

"This was a hit, Tee. They say it's M-16 and K shells scattered about out there."

"Them people still got it taped off?"

"Hell yeah."

"Congo, go out there for me. As soon as them people leave, call me. I'm coming out there."

"I know Special fucked up."

"Yeah, I gotta go see lil' sis, man."

"On my momma, somebody know somethin'."

"Yeah, I know. Too many shots rang out. Say, keep ole' girl that was renting them apartments with you once you get a hold of her. I wanna holla at her and see what nephew 'nem was on early in the a.m. that's all. Tell her I said not to let nobody up in there, a'ight? Love." I hung up, kissed Sharon and headed out to the Lac.

I rode to my sister crib, which took me all of ten minutes to get there. She stayed right out here on Palmer. When I got there, I noticed her car wasn't in the driveway. I knocked anyway just in case somebody else made a run in it.

"Special! Speciaaalll!" I yelled as I banged on the door.

I didn't get an answer. I wondered where she could be. I jumped back in the Lac and headed North to see what was up. I'd traveled about six blocks in that direction, when my pager started vibrating. It was the number Wolfy 'nem always paged me from. Only this time it had Congo's code behind it and 911. I hit a few blocks and dipped into a gas station to use the payphone.

When I got through, Congo answered. He told me though the police hadn't left, I needed to come to the block. He said Special was out there hysterical. She'd trampled the crime scene in a desperate attempt to see Lobo and Wolfy.

He said, "Some of y'all people out here but she ain't fuckin' wit' nobody! She's been callin' yo' name bruh."

I said, "Tell Special to give me five minutes. I'm on my way, a'ight?"

"A'ight," he replied, hanging up.

I felt sick, knowing I should've been there! I didn't wanna see them white folks' period.

*Why the fuck they still got the bodies out there?* I thought.

Being a known drug dealer, the police had been itchin' to pop me for anything they could. I'm the oldest out of us lil' niggas, and now that J.L. gone any criminal activity that occurred on the Northside had to have mine or Zoo's name written on it in their eyes. My hands would never be clean, but fuck 'em my sister needed me.

# Chapter 37

## *SOMEONE YOU LOVE*

When I made it to the hood, the scene was chaotic. Special was sitting Indian style in the middle of the street sobbing. Hundreds of people were out there that live on Burleigh. She wouldn't let anybody touch her. They were just watching her unfold. I walked up behind my little sister and scooped her up.

"No! N-o-o-o! Naaaw!" She kicked and screamed.

"It's me, Special, I'm here," I whispered in her ear.

She recognized my voice, instantly calming her soul. I carried her to my car and put her inside. Her words were barely audible.

All I could make out of all the gibberish she uttered, was, "My babies—Tee!"

Congo saw me grab her from amongst the crowd. He jogged over to the car, as me and the Homicide Detective Gina made eye contact. I saw her pointing in our direction while talking to another officer.

"What's up, bruh?" Congo greeted me with a handshake and a hug just as I'd closed Special in on the passenger's side. "I tried to console her man, but she—"

"It's a'ight now, I got her. I appreciate you, though," I told him. "I'm glad you called right away.

He said, "Oh, yeah! I got ole' girl Lalay over here wit' me. What you want me to do?"

"Do this for me, Congo, ask her if she was at home this morning when all the shootin' went down? See what she knows. You a big dude, be gentle with her. Try not to scare her. Let her know that I'm gon' look out for her. You are the only person she is to allow up in there until I can come get everything. Let her know we're just tryin' to get some answers. You still ain't heard from Proof 'nem?"

"Nall, I sure haven't," he replied.

"What's ole' girl's name? Damn, it's on the tip of my tongue wit' her fine ass."

"Who?" he asked.

"The one that used to mess with Kane, but she fuck wit' Proof now?"

"Oh, you talkin' about Deja?"

""Yeah, that's her. You got her number?"

"Nall, I ain't got her digits. She stays in the hood, though. Why, what's up?"

"Cause I need you to stop through there and see what's up with Proof for me. Then stop by Mighty's crib. His momma should be there if his girl ain't. If you go through there and ain't nobody seen or heard from them, have their families start callin' downtown and the hospitals. If them niggas happen to be at home laid up, tell them mutha—" I caught my temper. "Tell them dudes to get at me. I gotta take care of Special, man."

"A'ight," Congo replied.

I jumped in the car and smashed as the police approached us.

## Chapter 38

### *PROOF*

I was trying to pull off the impossible, which was to figure out a way to get Mighty out of the County before anybody found out he was down there. He'd had his girl Tameiko call me on three way this morning. They got him down there for Speeding, Driving Under The Influence, and the more serious charges were Suspicion Of Murder and Attempted Murder. Though he hadn't been officially charged, the local police, in a joint Task Force with the FBI were investigating. They were trying to tie his Chevy in with the shooting that we'd done on Eastside.

Somebody reported seeing a grey Chevy leaving the area. Mighty was suspected to have been involved in many of the city's unsolved murders and thought to be good for this one as well. The bullet holes in the car, along with the reports of the same make and model, had them convinced they finally had him. It's a good thing we'd dumped the guns in a garbage can in an alley on the East.

Otherwise, his recklessness may have made the case for the State that much easier. They had seventy-two hours to charge him, and time was ticking. He wanted me to put together twenty thousand, so when or if they dropped the hold on him, he could bond out. As soon as the sun goes down, I plan on going on a mission to get the guns and make sure they were properly destroyed. I had no idea we'd killed somebody. That's until this morning.

***

Pulling my dick out of my girl, I rolled over and answered the ringing phone.

I could tell by his tone, shit was deep. This is how our conversation went down, and how I had to decipher the code. Deja looked pissed when she handed me the phone.

"Who the fuck?" she griped.

"Hello!" I answered in a groggy and frustrating voice. *Who the fuck could be calling me over here?*

"Hello, is this Proof?" a female asked.

"Yeah, who the fuck is this!"

"This Tameiko. Mighty on the phone. Hold on. Mighty!"

"Yeah! Damn, girl! Stop all that hollerin'! He on?"

"Yeah, I'm here. What's up, Lawd? Where you at?" I sat up.

"Downtown. Meiko, put the phone down."

"She said, "A'ight! And y'all bet not be talkin' about no bitches either! If yo' ass would've been at home last night—"

"Girl, put the muthafuckin' phone down and let me holla at my nigga! Damn!" he snapped.

"All right! Dang, who you hollerin' at? Talkin' about me! Just call back if the phone hangs up. Bye!"

"Say, Lawd?" he sounded fucked up!

"Yeah, what happened?"

"They caught me speedin' down MLK. You ain't heard?"

I said, "Hell nall, I been at the crib."

"They holding me. Drunk, Speedin', but that's just a sting."

"Whatchu mean? What else they talkin' about?" I asked.

"Man, they down here talkin' some bullshit about some girls gettin' shot!"

"What? When, where at?" I acted surprised.

He said, "I don't know. Somewhere on the Eastside. I wasn't tryin' to hear none of that bullshit! I told them hillbillies to get me a mufuckin' pretender. I ain't did shit, don't know shit. So, we ain't have nothin' to rap about."

"So, you sayin' they tried to interrogate you?" I asked, to be clear.

"Yeah! They asked me about the bullet holes in the car. I told you my shit got shot up in front of the crib, right?"

I was caught off guard with that one. I didn't know the Chevy had bullet holes in it. It hadn't dawned on me until then that we hadn't checked before heading to the spot. I was still feeling tipsy when I answered the phone. But his words to me sobered my ass real quick. I played along with.it.

"Yeah, yeah! I remember."

What he was doing was puttin' it out there what they were coming at him with. I had to read between the lines.

"Well, they're tryin' to say somebody reported a Chevy like mine being like the one seen leaving the scene. It's a thousand grey Chevys out here riding around this bitch! They trippin'! But say, Lawd. Put twenty dollars together for me real quick. And go by that garbage ass bitch's house. Tell her I said to shoot her ass up here Sunday, or I'm through fuckin' wit' her ass."

That was code for, go get them guns or my ass is out! He loved Meiko's dirty panties. There was no way he was referrin' to her. Good thing she'd set the phone down. She more than likely would've snapped and fucked all that up.

Mighty had been in this predicament time and time again. He probably ain't trippin' but I am! Look what our drunken impaired actions led to. A girl is dead! Not what we'd planned by far. What if the hood finds out? Here I am in Deja's bedroom counting the money out one more time to be sure of what I had. It was damn near four in the evening, and I still wasn't where I wanted to be.

"Damn! I need five-thousand-seven-hundred more!" I yelled out of frustration. I'd been sneakin' around all morning, duckin' niggas collecting cash.

"Baby, you need money?" Deja asked.

I looked at her crazy because we hadn't been fuckin' that long. Plus, she'd never offered before. For a second, I wondered what had changed. Maybe it was me. I have been killin' that pussy on the regular lately.

"Yeah, I need fifty-seven hundred. Why, you got money?" I asked.

"Well, let's just say you don't need that anymore." She smiled.

"For real? You gon' give me fifty-seven hundred?" We heard a knock on the door downstairs."

She said, "Yeah, I can get that for you. I just came into a lil' somethin'. Hold up, let me see who this is at the door." She ran downstairs. I heard her yell, "Who is it!"

"It's Congo!" the voice from the other side replied.

Deja hollered for me before opening the door. "Proooffff!"

"Yeah!"

"Congo's here for you! Come on in, Congo." She stepped aside and let him in.

I immediately rushed down the stairs. I knew if this nigga was at the door, either Zoo or U-Tee had sent him. *Do they know?* I thought. Congo is also a traveler from the city.

"What's up, bruh?" I asked shaking up with him.

Have a seat. Deja went back upstairs. Congo, whose real name is Earl copped a seat taking me up on my offer. He took the couch, so I sat across from him.

The look on his face told me something was definitely wrong. "What's up, Lawd?" I asked again.

He leaned in and whispered, "Who's here?"

Nobody, just me and Deja. Why?"

He said, "Man, Joe, you ain't heard?" My heart sunk. "Lobo, Wolfy, Rise, Jungle and Mase got wet up on Burleigh this mornin'. Him and Zoo been hittin' you all mornin'. Where you been?"

"Damn, Lawd, for real? Hell nall I hadn't heard. Fuck!" I lied, pulling my pager from my hip pressing the buttons.

"My battery must be low. I ain't heard shit. My shit's dead. I ain't received no pages from nobody. Who did it? How bad is it?"

I'd been deliberately duckin' pages from Zoo and Tee, being that Mighty was locked up. I'd indeed heard about the murders.

He said, "Them niggas dead. Don't nobody know who did it. Whoever did that shit ain't leave nobody around to talk about it. I just talked to Lalay. She said she heard Lobo say something about some chicks wantin' to kick it. She says five minutes later they left out of the door. That's when she heard the shots. I ain't even told Tee yet. He tending to family, right now."

I was puttin' everything together in my head. Though I'd hoped like hell that U-Tee's nephews and my niggas, ain't have nothing to do with the bullshit we'd done. Common sense said it was a direct result. There hadn't been any shootings until we disturbed the peace and breached the agreement. The fact that we'd kept it a secret had just costed five of ours their lives.

Congo said, “You heard from Mighty?” He brought me out of a daze.

“Huh? Nall, I ain’t heard from ‘em.”

# Chapter 39

## *CONGO*

The only reason I asked the nigga had he heard from Mighty was because he was acting funny. Like he was somewhere else. Now, I'd just caught him in a lie. I didn't call 'em on it, though. Believe me, big homie saw everything. I'd just left Tameiko's crib lookin' for Mighty. She'd told me he was in jail, and that he'd called and talked to her and Proof this morning. I didn't even bother to ask her what he was down there for. I figured I'd just holla at Proof about it. Seeing this nigga sitting here lyin' like he ain't seen or heard from him had me thinkin'.

*Did they have something to do with lil' Folks nem gettin' their shit peeled back?*

There was a brief moment of silence, then I stood up to leave. "A'ight, Lawd." I shook Proof's hand. "Tee told me to tell you to get at him right away."

"For sure, I'm on that. You ain't been by Mighty crib?" he asked.

"Nall, but I'm gon' stop through there in a minute," I lied.

Fair exchange, I knew for a fact these young niggas stayed in some shit. They were the same way back home. Whatever they had goin' on, I was just tryin' to stay out of the way. Since Proof ain't trust me enough to tell me the truth, lets me know where we stand. The fact that we're all from the same projects and I'd known these brothers since they were runnin' around with snot coming out their noses went out of the window, I guess.

***

As soon as Congo left, I called Tameiko.

"Hello!" she finally answered, loud as hell like always.

"Hey, Meik, this Proof."

"Mighty still ain't—"

"I know, I know. Look, if Congo or anybody else comes by there, you ain't seen Mighty, a'ight?"

"Boy, you too late. Congo came by here about a half hour ago."

"Damn, he did?" He'd lied to me.

"Yup, he knows Mighty's in jail. He said he was comin' over there next. Guess he ain't made it. I wasn't supposed to—"

"Damn, a'ight Tameiko. Thanks." I slammed the phone down. I had a lot of decisions to make.

# Chapter 40

## *Mighty*
## *U Was My Nigga Now We Beefin'*

Once I hung up the phone, I went right back to my cell. It was almost time for them to start servin' chow anyway. This County jail shit is fucked up! They ain't got shit on me, though. A description of a car ain't enough to file no charges. At least, that's what I was thinkin' when I walked back into the slave cage.

"Who was that on the phone, nigga, wifey? You been on that horn all mornin'." the nigga Minkah questioned as he sat on the top bunk. He's my celly, a good dude. I know some of his people out in the world.

"Hell yeah," I replied. "I just had her hit my nigga. Everything should be good now. It's times like these that a nigga wished he was back home."

Minkah said, "Aw shit, here we go. All you Chicago cats run that same shit when these people in Wisconsin get a hold of you. All I ever hear is y'all come this way to get money. It's sweet."

"Nigga it is sweet." I smiled.

"This time they handin' niggas ain't!" he replied with a straight face. "It don't taste shit like honey to me. And never forget this, young dog. It ain't where you from. It's where you at." He tapped his temple with his right index finger. He said, "It's plenty of money in Chicago. Why you runnin' from it, huh?"

"You about to eat this bullshit they servin' for lunch?" I asked.

He said, "Hell nall."

"Me neither, I guess I can run it down to you then. I ain't really here because a nigga wanna be. Trust me, I ain't one of them niggas! You got me fucked up."

"And what nigga is that?" the old head asked.

"One of them runnin' ass niggas. Niggas that can't go back home. I still be through that bitch Windy! Though it's probably best for me to never go home again. I'm a creature of habit, I guess. I remember you said something along those lines this morning when they brought me in."

He said, "You right, I said it because you're constantly comin' in and out of here on a regular."

"I ain't worried about it. These people can't trap me, keep me or eat me."

He said, "That's where you're wrong. You've yet to enter a maximum institution. So, you've got no idea how this system can literally swallow you whole. You've never seen the belly of the beast."

"I ain't tryin' to hear none of that shit. I don't plan on goin' But, you're right, I've came close. Guess I'll have to tell you about this particular hoe-ass nigga, and why I'm living in exile instead of being home with my people. Aw, he was a killa! But so am I, belly of the beast."

I laughed. "I'm the only beast I know. Damn, I still miss Amesha."

*I almost went to prison! All over a bitch, fuckin' wit' my nigga out the hood. Me and this nigga Treefa had been shootin' it out for weeks! I was out of breath. The fag had just chased me out of the McDonald's drive-thru bussin' at me! Of course, I had to dump back! I left the trap though and hit it on foot. I still remember it like it was yesterday. I was at the payphone outside the liquor store on Roosevelt and Independence. I dialed her number. As soon as she answered, I snapped!*

*"Hello?" she answered, with that country sass I've always loved.*

*"Mesh, I'm killin' yo' muthafuckin' brother!"*

*"Wha-what! Who is dis!" she asked, playin' stupid."*

*"Bitch, this Mighty! You know my muthafuckin' voice!"*

*"Whatchu talkin' about! What happened! You ain't gon—"*

*"What the fuck you think happen! The nigga just got at me again! Again, over my shit!" She'd so-called squashed the beef we'd been goin' through.*

*She said, "You shouldn't have—"*

*I hung up on her ass.*

Yeah, it was a little more to it than I was leadin' on. See, I used to fuck with Mesha. But it's sad to say, the shit wouldn't end with me and this nigga until one of us was dead. Mesha was my first love. Before I loved the money. Before I loved the streets. Before I loved anything I thought loved me back.

We'd met back in elementary. From then on, middle school through high school we were together. Day one, she was mine and I was hers. We'd said forever. Her honey-chocolate skin, prominent cheek bones and bright brown eyes lit up my world. Her perfectly shaped nose, beautiful smile and gorgeous lips did something to me that has yet to be done again.

Actually, I couldn't picture myself without her. She was my everything. All I ever needed, I could easily choose her again. She was headstrong, the body was bangin' and the pussy was sweeter than brown sugar to my tongue. Back then, me and my niggas called ourselves Nike Boyz, *Niggaz Iz Killin' Everything!*

The homies grew a lil' salty at me for a minute, though. I rarely had time to fuck with them. These were the times, where if you saw me, you saw Mesh. I couldn't have her around all the bullshit that came with the game, so I kept my distance at times. Don't get me wrong. I was there when we had to ride or make money moves here and there. But I was in love and love conquers all. I guess Tree was in love, too. Everything was good. We was gettin' guap. I had my queen, life was sweet. That's until Amina Bills started attending Deuce Sabel with us. Mina was beautiful! Most likely, she still is. She stood about 5'5, with cocoa butter skin, a nice body and a thick mane. Yeah, she was a sweetie pie.

Her arrival caused somewhat of a fiascal, but wit' Mesh by my side, and dollar signs in my eyes, I paid little or no attention to her. She'd already had more than half the niggas at school tryin' to get at her. In the end, she ended up with my nigga Tree.

After my dude Proof left, me and this dude became aces. He's the one that introduced me to Mesh. She's his sister! So, yeah, we went back like Chico-sticks, Boston Baked Beans and Jolly Joe's!

You feel me? We'd kilt shit, built shit and tore shit down! So, the first time this nigga, *my brother* pulled his gun on me! It hurt! He knew the rules. You pull that muthafucka out, you better use it! It's a code amongst killaz and that's how shit got crazy.

We could've busted each other's heads, messed up each other's faces and still been there to shake hands. I ain't mean to fuck his bitch. Nah, it wasn't even like that. See, what had happened was this.

One night we'd all went out. Every nigga was with me, besides Tree. I figured him and his woman was together. But there she was. In the club puttin' all that ass on me. She knew I was practically married. A' nigga was drunk and higher than a giraffe's pussy! I can't lie, though, my hands roamed places they shouldn't have. A few of my niggas approached us, askin' what we were on?

True was the last to bring it to me. He said, "Lawd, you trippin'. You should step outside and get some air." He started pulling me away from Mina.

I'd did just that. It was winter and the fresh air was bringin' a nigga down. Then, here she comes again, with all her intoxication. She'd followed me out there.

She said, "Mighty, what's up? You just gon' leave? Who else am I supposed to dance wit' up in there? Oh, it's cold." She wrapped her arms around me, laying her head on my chest. "Keep me warm." she said.

## Chapter 41

### *My Homeboy's Girlfriend*

She was lookin' up at me with those beautiful, dark-brown eyes and that's when I saw it. That light, that twinkle every woman I've ever met has in her eyes when she's decided she's gonna give me that pussy. So, I held her. It was damn near closing time, and with people comin' out of the club it wasn't a good look for either of us. So, I told her we could sit in my car under the heat until her friends came out. We'd waited a few minutes, when she'd decided to say fuck 'em. She was ready to leave them. She asked if I could drop her off. I'd rode solo, so it wasn't a problem. When we finally got to her crib, she asked me if I wanted to come in for what she referred to as a *nightcap*. I'd never heard the term used before.

So, I asked, "What the hell is that?"

She said, "A drink stupid."

Thinkin' with my third leg, I went in. One thing led to another, and we ended up gettin' it in rough! After the nut, we both knew we were wrong. It should've ended there but it didn't. We'd fucked weekly for almost two years before it winded up gettin' back to Tree. The chemistry was so strong, I guess we'd gotten sloppy somehow. Tree—lord knowing everything about me, my spots ended up gettin' hit. The only reason I figured out he was behind the shit was his mouth. A few weeks after a muthafucka hit the spots, somebody ran in my tilt.

We were all out in The Gardens kickin' it at NeNe's crib. She's one of the home girls from around the way.

We were all out there watching Sugar Ray thrash somethin'. We had a bunch of liquor and weed floating around her spot, gettin' fucked up? Mina and Mesha were both there. Actually, we all had a piece off in that joint. Lord was actin' strange and real stand-of-fish.

He was sayin' shit like, "Mighty, that's how I'll beat that ass nigga! Ha-haaa!" He knew, we ain't never played like that!

I just said, "Oh, yeah?" I was lookin' upside his head, since he didn't have the nuts to look at me.

He said, "Hell yeah, nigga! We can put the gloves on and place a small wager on that shit." We made eye contact.

Then he said, "But that last seventy-five thousand you just lost probably set shit back for you, huh?" You probably need to regroup, my nigga." He stuffed face with nachos.

See, that's where he'd fucked up. I'd never told niggas how much a muthafucka got out of my crib. So, that sent the antennas straight through the roof! It was a definite red flag. I kept it cool, though. Shit was starting to add up in my head. This nigga was always calling me enquiring about my whereabouts.

I said, "We don't need the gloves, Lawd. We can go outside right now if you want to. Don't let this shit on TV hype you up to the point where you feel like yo' hands better than mine. You know better," he snapped.

"What the fuck you mean, I know better, nigga? Fuck all this talkin' shit! Let's go outside! I been waitin' to holla at you 'bout somethin' anyway! On the fin!"

"Oh!" Dola instigated. "Y'all serious? Y'all serious, Lawd?"

He said, "Hell yeah, we're serious! Let's holla then, nigga!"

# Chapter 42

## *Many Men Wish Death Upon Me*

I got up, the ladies began to protest, tellin' us to chill. This nigga had his chest poked out, like he was gon' smash me! We headed out as everybody followed. It was time. As we hit the stairs, it started comin' out. A couple of the brothers tried to holla at 'em.

He said, "Fuck that, snake ass nigga! You ain't think I was gon' find out!" He had niggas lookin' at me sideways. I ain't say shit, though, I just shrugged.

The guilt was immediate. Pin asked me, "What's he talkin' about, Lawd?"

I just looked at 'em. We'd made it outside. Everybody encircled us. He came at me on some drunk shit, swingin' wild. He threw a haymaker. I side stepped it and hit 'em in his mouth. He stumbled, and I smelled blood. When I stepped toward him to finish 'em, he upped, pointin' a .45 at me!

"Whoa!" I stepped back, in disbelief.

"Hold on! Lord, whatchu doin'!" Bug grabbed him from behind.

His gun burst causing everybody to scatter. As Bug lifted him off his feet in a bear hug, he kept bussin', bullets started ricocheting off the concrete.

He yelled, "Nigga fuckin' my bitch!"

I wasn't even strapped! So, I headed back in the building to get my shit! I came back out wit' whop, niggas grabbin' on me and shit.

"Lawd! Laaawd, he's gone!" Big Dola finally got my attention.

He said, "Y'all niggas out here trippin'! Y'all brothers! You know y'all out of order!" He was pissed, but so was I.

Mesha was still out there, though. I hadn't meant for her to find out like that. In all the bullshit that was goin' down, she'd whipped Mina, and then ran up on me.

"Mighty, so y'all fuckin'! You and that bitch fuckin'!"

"Nah, Mesh," I lied.

"That's what the fuck my brother just said! She ain't denied the shit!" She muffed me, then pushed me.

She knew I wouldn't hit her. So, the gun in my hand was invisible to her.

Pointing her finger at me, she said, "I gotcho muthafuckin' ass! That all right! I got you." Tears flooded her face.

She said, "I'm through with you!" She walked off, and I felt my heart break.

"Mesh! Amesha!" I called after her. She wasn't tryin' to hear it, though.

She'd stopped taking my calls. When she saw me at school, she went the other way. I was sick! In the Jects news travels fast. The next day, a few niggas came at me talkin' about how Treefa had been bragging about gettin' me for a couple hundred thousand. It ain't do shit but confirm what I already knew. I was lookin' for Tree-Lord and niggas knew it. He couldn't duck me forever. He's from where I'm from. All I wanted was my money back, and to get back right with my baby.

A week later, I spotted him gettin' off the El down on 22$^{nd}$ So, I hollered out to 'em, "Tree, what's up, nigga!"

He turned around, upped, and got to dumpin'!

*Lak! Lak! Lak! Lak! Lak! Lak! Lak! Lak!*

Niggas tried to get down on me, again! We both had tools this time, though, so it went up. A few innocent bystanders winded up gettin' hit in the exchange. But I'd missed him, and he'd missed me. Every time we saw each other from then on, the results were the same. There wouldn't be any sleep until shit was permanent. A lot of shells had been spent.

Niggas loved us both. Some took my side, but to me it seemed as though the majority had taken his. I felt like niggas were wishin' me dead. They'd vowed not to get involved, being it would've started an all-out war amongst our own.

# Chapter 43

## *Redemption*

Out of nowhere, I started hearing that Amesha was tryin' to get in touch with me. I didn't know what she was on, until I went and talked to her. She told me she'd talked to her brother, and he'd agreed to give my money back and squash the bullshit. I told her that was cool. To have Lord call me.

That was the night before last. Then, the nigga tried to take my head off with an AK-47 while I was ordering a Big Mac and some fries. So, I guess I couldn't eat either.

I got up with some of the brothers from RG, and they set it up for me and him to meet up the next day outside of the buildings. Shit was supposed to be peaceful. When I arrived everybody was out there. Bad ass kids, niggas my age to the old folks. Tree-lord included the nigga was actually smiling when I walked up. I knew that smile, though. It ain't mean shit. I'd seen him murder niggas wearing that same face many days. I'd put a smile on just to comfort him, but I couldn't chance it. I wouldn't miss again.

I walked up to him and shook his hand. While still grasping his palm, I blew his brains out. His body collapsed, but his grip remained firm. He'd gone into shock. I shook him off me and ran off into the night. His blood spatter was all over me. I went home, changed and slept like a baby.

The next day, I was charged with First Degree Intentional Homicide. Mesha told The Twelves everything; about me and Mina! Treefa takin' my money, us gettin' it up as far as the fight. And, the shootouts! The call I'd placed threatening his life made me their number one suspect. I'd sat in Cook County for damn near two years, before The District Attorney dismissed the charges without prejudice, being there were no witnesses willing to come forward. There was no gun, no nothing. All they had was the word or an ex-fiend, who said I'd cheated on her with her friend. I damn sure wasn't about to stick around and let 'em build a case on me. I got the fuck up outta Chicago! They say, out of sight out of mind. Well, how about out of state out of mind?

I called Proof and got on the first thing smokin'. That's how a nigga landed in Wisconsin. When I do go back home, it's behind tint. Layin' real low. I'm in and out, murder for hire. Iz! A nigga still killin' errythang!

# Chapter 44

## *SIX*
## *Family Affair*

A few days had passed, and it was finally time for Honesty to be released from the hospital. I had just finished packing her car. I was escorting her from the building when two white men approached us in the parking lot.

"Excuse me, Ms. Honesty Brown?" one of them asked, glancing briefly at a photograph of her on a piece of paper, then back at her.

"Yes? I'm Honesty," she replied.

He cleared his throat. "Sorry to bother you. My God, we almost missed you. I'm Agent Dyer. This is my partner, Agent Chamberlin." The other simply nodded. "We need to ask you—"

"She ain't got nothin' to say to y'all. Let's go, Hon," I interrupted.

Honesty turned her back to them and continued toward the car with the FBI following closely behind.

"Ms., we just wanna ask you if you're familiar with or know a Michael Turner aka, Mighty Mike?"

"Who?" Honesty turned back toward them.

"Michael Turner," Chamberlin repeated, stepping forward. "He was being held—"

"Never heard of him," I said sternly, as I opened Honesty's door.

"He's right, I can't say I've ever heard the name before," she said as I held her hand and eased her inside the car.

I then reached around her, grabbed her seatbelt and buckled her in. As I shut the door, I was heated, and she could tell. I walked around the car, sneering at the Feds.

"Stupid muthafiuckas! This how y'all do it? This the procedure, huh!"

Honesty rolled down the window. She said, "Bae, let's just go!" She knew I was strapped, so I needed to be cool.

I shook my head at the suited government officials and got in the car and pulled off. The mention of Mighty's name had my blood boiling. Me and 3C wanted to set Burleigh on fire with shells every night until we caught up with Proof since Mighty was in jail. The only thing keeping us from it was Doe. Although it took him hours to convince us that going back would be a trap and a one-way ticket to the pen, he'd done it. The five murders had shit hot.

He and Moo found it peculiar that Zoo hadn't sent shooters right back East. Or anywhere else in the city for that matter. They felt something was up and asked 3C to fallback until shit cooled off. Then, here comes these fag-ass Alphabet Boys tryin' to scare the shit out of Honesty before I could even get her home.

That's when I had my light bulb moment, in replaying what they'd said. The Agent said the nigga Mighty *was* being held.

*That means he's out!* I thought.

# Chapter 45

## *You Must Love Me*

"Six, so, this Mighty Michael dude or whatever. Is he the one that shot up my house?" Honesty questioned as we rode.

"Uh-uh, we ain't never heard of the nigga. Remember?" I replied, grabbing her hand. "Just chill. Let me take you home, a'ight? And by the way you moved." I smiled.

"I moved? What you mean, I moved?" Honesty asked.

"I told you I was going to take care of everything, I couldn't have you tryin' to go back over there and live. You ain't mad, are you?"

"Nall, not at all. I'm just surprised you did it all in such a short time. Do my momma know?"

"Yeah, Ma-Duke knows. I gave her the money. She helped me get the apartment. It's in her name. I bought you brand new everything. Living room, dining, kitchen and bathroom sets."

"Shut up, boy! No, you didn't?" She wore a huge smile.

"Yup, I even got you a new TV and a stereo. Plus, a new wardrobe, with shoes pumps and all. The girls helped me shop."

"Stop playin', boi!" She punched me in my upper right arm. I laughed. "You playin' right?" She gave me another two- piece.

"Oww! Ahh!" I winced playfully. "Nah, I'm serious. Don't worry, though. I ain't throw nothin' away. I put everything in storage in case you wanted to keep some of the stuff from your old crib."

"Oh, thank you, thank you!" She kissed me on the cheek as I drove, causing me to swerve.

"Aye, chill out. You gon' fuck around and make a nigga crash. Hey, Pookie at the crib, too. I asked her to come do your hair. So, her and your momz there now."

"Whatchu sayin', my hair nappy or somethin'?" she asked, twirling her bang in her finger.

"Nah, what I'm sayin' is you need ya shit done," I joked.

"It's been damn near a week." I looked over at her, smiling.

"Fa-get chu!" She poked out her bottom lip and punched me.

"Ah! You gon' stop beatin' on me then tryin' to kiss me, too?" I laughed.

"Where everybody else at?" she questioned.

"Shit, I don't know. I guess you'll have to ask Pookie. I'm sure they'll all come around once they know you're home."

"You're right, I do need my shit whipped," she said looking in the visor mirror above the dash.

When I pulled up to the entrance of the underground parking garage, she went crazy.

"'Six! Marcus, oh—wee. You got me a place in the Arcade building?"

These apartments sit on the lake. They're plush, like the places they be showing on TV in New York. High ceilings, and big bay windows. The place is more like a luxury hotel with elevators, security cameras and doors, carpet and wooden floors, the works. It cost a bundle to stay by the white folks. Honesty was so used to the hood. She'd heard stories about the Arcade.

"Yup, I told you I gotchu." I grinned as I pulled in the driveway.

She was in awe; she couldn't believe it. When they stepped off the elevator and got on the hallway, I handed her the keys.

"It's this way," I told her.

We walked hand and hand until we got to apartment three-thirteen.

I stopped, "Here it is, I hope you like it. You should, your shit is better than mine."

"I know I will." She hugged me tightly, kissed my lips and thanked me again.

She took a deep breath, inserted the key and unlocked the door. She stepped in yelling for her mother.

Everybody greeted her, welcoming her home. Camera flashes had her stuck like a deer caught in the glare of headlights. She froze, a single tear ran down her face. Everybody was there, Moo, Doe, 3C and family.

As she looked around, she said, "Awww, my hair!" She grabbed her head.

Honesty was laughing and crying at the same time. Pookie said, "I gotchu, sis." She walked over to Honesty and hugged her, everybody else followed suit.

Honesty cried mixed tears of joy, sorrow and pain. She was happy to be alive. Happy to see her loved ones and her crew. But there was a hole in her chest that would never heal. Someone was missing and would forever be missed, Autumn.

As she and her auntie Sherry hugged, she knew she had a funeral to attend and the family would never the same.

She said, "Auntie, thank you for comin'. You must love me."

Sherry said, "Baby, it's not your fault. Just promise me y'all gon' get them niggas."

Honesty said, "I promise you!"

# Chapter 46

## *PROOF*

Mighty swerved up on the block and jumped out. He'd been out of jail for two days, but this was the first time anybody from the hood had seen him.

"On the fin, lawd! What's up?" he asked, as he shook up with me, Reez and Smacks.

We were standing out on the corner. It was a quiet night, but this nigga was drunk, strapped and ready to pop somethin'.

"Where you been, nigga?" Reezly asked.

"Laid up, lil' nigga," Mighty replied.

I said, "We ain't on shit. Just waiting on some money to slide through."

"What's up, Joe?" Smacks greeted him. "I got somthin' stupid, right now. Ready to plug some donuts they come through this bitch!" He raised his shirt, showing off the .45 he had tucked in his belt.

Reez said, "Me too!" He clutched a .357 Mag.

"Awe, yeah?" Mighty smiled. "Y'all wanna do it to 'em? Why they gotta come through here? We can hop in the trap right now and—" He pulled two Billy Dee's of his own. He was rockin' two Colt .45s.

"Hold on, Lawd!" I interjected. "Mighty, let me holla at you for a second! Y'all wildin'! Put that shit up!"

"What's up, Lawd?" He mean mugged me. "Holla at me. Y'all lil' niggaz gon' jump in the car." He nodded toward the Short booty 9-8 he'd just pulled up in.

Reez and Smacks looked at me. "Go head!" Mighty told them.

They smiled, wasting no time running for the car as Mighty tucked his weapons.

"Hey-hey-hey! Don't touch my sounds!" he yelled.

I said, "What—the-fuck nigga! I just had my girl post a dub to get yo' ass out! I ain't seen yo' muthafuckin' ass and you come out here on this bullshit! You know if Zoo finds out we—"

"Chill nigga, damn! He ain't gon' find shit out unless you| tell em. I got these lil niggaz." He smiled.

"You got— nigga is you crazy! You can't be—" Mighty waved me off, walking toward the car. He looked over his shoulder.

"I take it you ain't comin'? We'll be back in a minute. We gon' ride East? Then, we gon' swing up through the ghetto on our way back! See if anybody out there that I don't like! You forgettin' where we from, huh? You getting soft on me, Lawd?" He shook his head.

"Mighty! Mighty!" I tried to stop 'em, but he ignored me. He jumped in the car, looked at me and turned up the bangs. When he started recruiting niggas like Congo and True to come to the Mil, I should've known it was gon' be some bullshit.

*Here's a lil somthin' 'bout a nigga like me/Never shoulda been let out the penitentiary/Ice cube would like to say/That I'ma crazy muthafucka from around the way/Since I was a youth/I smoked weed out/Now I'm the muthafucka that you read about—*

He smashed off, throwing up Vice Lord. I watched and listened, as the sounds and the taillights faded in the distance. They'd turned the corner. "Nigga, we ain't back home." I mumbled to myself, as I strolled to the crib.

# Chapter 47

## *MIGHTY*

I'm from the Westside, off Jackson and Rockwell in The City. For all you slow niggaz that's Chicago. I came up under Dola, Chess, Bug and a long line of killaz. No pops, momma a dope fiend. Shit it got rough early! What y'all know about heatin' up the crib with the stove? No food in the refrigerator cause momz done sold everything! The food stamps! The TV, the cable box, our clothes, her ass and her soul to the pipe! Not much, huh? What a muthafucka know about canned goods, syrup sandwiches? No meat between the bread just sugar! Government cheese and raw ass hotdogs? Cockroaches and rats that'll bite niggaz!

Cause it wasn't nothin' else around for 'em to chew on! You ever cried yourself to sleep behind the hunger pangs? Nah, I ain't think so. So, before you go judging a nigga about the route I took! Or preach some shit about a Jesus lovin' me! Hold ya breath. No more lies! Ain't nobody gave a fuck about me from the day I was born. To the streets! To all the Lil Yummys out there. We strive. To the chiefs and legends! H-Town, L-Town, The Holy City! The Black Gates, to Moe-Town, $43^{rd}$, $55^{th}$ and niggaz off O-Block!

Though I ain't there, I ain't forgot. The Gardens! You are what you are, so it is what it iz! Almighty! See, my first thoughts and dreams when shit went bad was to kill all them bitches! Any nigga that served Fienna Turner. That's until I talked to the big homie about the shit. He gave me a different vision. Lord gave me a plan. I was only eight years old when Dola put that first pistol in my hands.

I remember lookin' at the steel, thinkin', *'Damn, this mufucka heavy. Lookin' at the packs like, this it? This is what she loved more than me!*

So, it begins, I knew exactly how to start rackin' shit. It was right there in my face every day anyways. I became the men I'd hated. I started serving my momma.

In turn, she started bringing me clientele throughout the buildings. Niggaz was trying to tell me I was wrong! Fuck them niggaz! They was just mad cause they wasn't catchin' that good Fie-money no more. That's my momma! My nigga Proof was staying a few doors down from me. He was going through the same shit I was with his momz city, so I put him in. It wasn't long before we were outside in front of the buildings with the older niggaz. Big Dola made sure we was straight. Him, Bug, Chess and the rest of them niggaz stayed out there deep. Whatever my momma didn't help us get off, they made sure it was sold.

After a few years, Proof's momma wised up. I could only hope mine did the same, followed suit and got clean. I guess it was all on me, though. Being I was right there in the crib with her and the dope. To be sure she wouldn't relapse and fall to her old ways, she moved her and my nigga out of the state! She said, fuck just leaving the hood. He'd come back and visit from time to time. Other than that, we stayed in touch over the jack. I had to let 'em know how we was comin' up!

By the time I was fifteen, I was knee deep in the game. I had a squad of lil niggaz runnin' up under me. Dola that nigga! He made sure every one of us had our own pistols, and our own Ks. Imagine fifteen lil niggaz runnin' around the Gardens with that shit! He also made sure we all had our own Chevys' once we were old enough to drive. No paint, no rims, but they were ours. All that other shit would come.

He taught us how to screen niggas comin' through Rockwell that didn't belong. If you weren't with somebody that stayed in them buildings or known to be out there, wasn't shit shakin'. You wasn't just, comin' through cause you so-called claimed that five-point star. We ain't give a fuck how old you were neither. Them lil niggaz gon' be the ones with the choppaz! We call the police Twelves.' Even when they rolled through, Chess and the other brothers let it be known that they had to move the fuck around. Sendin' shots at the squads made that clear as day. Bug, Lawd was the Mastermind behind the money. It was his connect that kept the projects flooded.

We brought in some serious money as young niggas. Our teachers wouldn't see what we were making a week in an entire year! You couldn't tell me nothin' so, I probably wasn't listening when a nigga told me. Though we rise, some will surely fall. I should've known shit wouldn't always be so smooth along the way. You know, when you makin' noise, eatin' good and fuckin' good, certain niggas ain't gon' like that. All I know is what my niggas told me and showed me. A lot of people say it ain't no hope for me. They blame my momma for bringin' me up this way. For introducin' me to certain shit. But, hold on. Let me cock my shit.

It's some ops out here on 10th Street. We about to drill some holes in these niggaz. Fuck they doin' out here! Niggaz know they supposed to head home when it gets dark! Knowin' the monster Mighty on the loose.

"Y'all lil' niggaz ready? We jumpin' out!" Smacks smiled.

Reez cocked the .357, the car came to a stop.

***

A few Goonies were posted and out on the grind when we came to an abrupt stop and the doors flew open. We jumped out of the blue Nine-Eight in our signature colors, hats banged to the left.

Lil Terror, Baby G, and World scattered seeing the guns in our hands. They tried to run for cover.

*Boom! Booom! Boomm!*

"Don't run, bitch! Come here!" I yelled, hitting World in his shoulder and his back causing him to damn near flip as he hit the pavement.

*Bak! Bak!* Lil Terror got off two shots.

*Booom! Booom! Boooom! Boom! Boom! Boom! Boommm!*

Smacks and Reez busted their guns at G and Terror. G got hit in his ass as he dipped through the cut. Terror got away barely uninjured. As the Nine-Eight idled in the middle of the street, I walked up to World and shot him in his head as he squirmed up the sidewalk.

Reez and Smacks had already jumped back in the car. I casually walked back to the trap, looping around the hood, I got in the driver's seat, closed the door and adjusted the rearview mirror. Then I ejected the N.W.A. tape and put a dub in that Chess had just sent me from back home. This was some up-and-coming underground niggas out of Texas named Gheto Boys. I turned up the volume all the way up.

As I pulled away slowly, I bobbed my head and yelled over the music. "Now we gotta ride through the North. Fire that weed up!"

*This how I started lil niggaz! I started small time dope game cocaine/ Pushin' rocks on the block/ I'm never broke mane.*

I smiled, rapping Face's lyrics to the anthem.

# Chapter 48

## *CONGO*
## *So Many Tears*

It was a gloomy Thursday morning due to rain, and The First Baptist Church was jammed packed. Wisconsin Avenue was crowded with mourners that wouldn't be able to get in for attendance. Funeral services for sixteen and seventeen-year-old Wolfy and Lobo was in session. The North side came out to pay their respects.

Wails could be heard for blocks outside the church, as Reverend McGee called to the heavens over their souls. "They with God now! I say, they're with God now. Can I get a Amen?" He dabbed the sweat from his brow as he preached on.

Special had cried so many tears, they would no longer form. She was drained with grief.

"Sister Special gon' need you, Lord! She gon' need just to cover her with the blood of The Lamb! Wrap your arms around her! Give her strength! God, you said in Isaiah chapter fifty-eight, verse eleven that you would make us strong! Lord we need you now! Lord in Mathew chapter nineteen, verses fourteen and fifteen you said the Kingdom of Heaven belongs to the children! Place your hands upon them Lord. In verse twenty-six, He said, with God! Again, I say with God, all things are possible, Amen?"

Amens could be heard throughout the Church.

"You know, I baptized Willie and Lamont in this here church! They'd been coming to this church for some time as little babies. But they were led astray Lord. Led astray by them streets. See, the church sees it all. God hears and sees everything! In His church here on earth, we hear and see a lil', too."

"Gone Reverend!" somebody yelled from the pews.

"Oh, yeah! I'm seeing a lot of y'all up in here that done disappeared from the church. Um-hmm, I sees ya, and I've got a message for you! See, you done turned to them streets like Lamont and Willie! God has put on my heart to tell you, while I've got this here opportunity!"

"In the name of Jeeesus!" some lady yelled.

"See, y'all don't wanna do nothing but sell dope and kill," The Reverend said.

Zoo, U-Tee, Proof and Mighty couldn't help but think he was speaking directly to them. The Reverend made eye contact with each and every one of them as he spoke.

He said, "Proverbs six-six-seventeen says, You people don't want to work! Think about the ant! Consider its ways to be wise! See there, even the ant gotta work! It says, it has no commander! It has no leader or ruler!" The Reverend looked directly at Zoo as he quoted these words, "But he stores food in the summer! You lazy people, how long will you lie there? When will you get up from your sleep?

"You might sleep or take a little nap! You might fold your hands and rest! Then you would feel poor, as if somebody robbed you! Don't sleep on GOD!" The Reverend dabbed his face. "Satan will rob you! He says, a worthless and evil man says things with his mouth.

"He winks his eyes. He makes signals with his feet!" The Reverend stomped a few feet away from the podium. "He motions with his fingers! He has lies in his heart! Look here, this book is good! The Word says, he who is always stirring up fights, trouble will catch up to him in an instant! He will suddenly be destroyed! Nothing can save him," he lowered his voice.

"It says here, there are six things the Lord hates. In fact, there are seven. The Lord hates proud eyes, a lying tongue, and hands that kill those who are not guilty." As he looked at Mighty and Proof, they both had the same thought running through their minds.

*Who the fuck been talkin' to this nigga?*

# Chapter 49

## *TELESIS*
## *Cuz I Love You*

Ironically, on the Eastside of town, Autumn's service was also being held. Honesty stood before the church in tears, as she recited a poem that she'd written the night before, entitled *Autumn*.

She said, "Dear Autumn. My cousin, my sister, my heart, my joy. I long for the days you'd knock at my door. Who is it, I'd yell! And you'd say, Autumn. I'll keep you forever, in my heart and my dreams. And I promise, as long as I live, you'll live through me. It's Honesty, by blood we're bonded. We danced, we laughed, we rapped, we sang. If blessed with a daughter, her name shall be, Autumn. A smile as wide, and big as the ocean. Bright as leaves in the forest in the month of October. We love you, and we'll be missing you, Autumn. You came. You—you caame! I-I'm sorry—" Honesty broke down and was unable to finish.

Six and her mother rushed to her side as she rested her head on the podium. As she cried, Debra rubbed her back and whispered in her ear.

"Honesty, baby you alright? Can you finish?" She shook her head. "Well, come on. It's alright, she knows you love her."

She raised her head, she and her mother hugged. Six then guided them back to their seats. The church stood and gave Honesty a round of applause.

The Pastor grabbed the mic and said, "Amen."

God works in mysterious ways at times. And this was another way of showing it. It turns out the two sides of town would bump heads at Union Cemetery, since it is the most common ground for black folks to be laid to rest in the city. The funerals taking place on the same day, made it fate that we'd see each other.

"Yo', Doe," Moo whispered. "Ain't that them niggas Mighty and Proof over there?" Doe looked.

"Yeah, the nigga Zoo, too. Pull Thirty over here real quick before Six sees this shit," Doe replied.

Moo turned to his left. "Telesis, tap Thirty. Tell him to come step over here for a sec," Moo whispered as the Pastor eulogized and all were in tears.

I delivered the message, Thirty and Tank came and stood next to Moo, Doe and Jahnahdah.

"Y'all seein' this shit?" Doe asked in a low tone.

Tank said, "Yeah man, shit's wild. What the fuck they doin' here?"

Thirty said, "Today of all days, huh? I guess it happens sometimes when you've got death in such close proximity of each other."

Six hadn't noticed, because he was Honesty's legs. Her bereavement had her in a state where she could barely stand. It never really hits you, until the funeral and the burial.

Tank said, "I'm knowin' big Six-hunnid ain't seen this shit! You think we should tell 'em?"

Moo said, "Yeah, go whisper in his ear while I make sure everybody else on point. Tell 'em to stay calm and remember where we at."

Doe said, "There's a time and place for everything, and this ain't it. I think Zoo got enough sense to let us bury ours in peace if we're willin' to let him bury his. They seein' us, just as we're seein' them."

"A'ight. Let me go holla at him," Thirty replied.

# Chapter 50

## *THIRTY*
## *Cocky And Confident*

I approached Six as he stood behind Honesty in the front row with the family. Standing next to him, I whispered in his ear while staring at our enemies. "Don't turn around, my nigga. But them niggas Proof and Mighty behind you on the other side of the yard. About fifty feet away."

Six reached for his waist, but Tank stepped in out of nowhere and grabbed his arm.

"Honesty, her momma and all these other women and kids out here, bruh," Tank whispered.

I said, "They're attending a funeral. We'll get em. But this is not the time nor place. Just nod if you understand."

Tank said, "Stay calm, a'ight."

Six dropped his head and took his hand off his thrilla. He didn't say a word. He simply nodded.

Tank let go of his arm. "Good. Stay here with Honesty. Don't worry about nothin'. I'm gon' see if Doe nem will let me go holla at them niggas before we leave." Tank extended his fist.

There was a moment's hesitation, then Six gave him a pound.

When we got back to where the men were standing, Jah overheard Moo mention niggas leaving and him wanting to go holla.

Jahnahdah said, "Doe, y'all bet not start no shit out here."

"We aint," Moo shot back. "Tank, you and Thirty come with me. I wanna holla at these niggaz Zoo and U-Tee myself," Moo said, heading in their direction.

U-Tee and his family were heading to their limousines when Zoo' heard Moo call out to. him. When they turned to see us approaching, Tee told his family to go ahead of them. Mighty and Proof stepped out in front of Zoo and U-Tee and drew their weapons. Me and Tank went to draw ours, but Moo stopped us.

"Whoa! Hold on. We come in peace." Moo smiled. "I just wanna holla at Zoo and U-Tee real quick.

"Do I know you?" U-Tee questioned.

"Nah, I know *of* you," Moo replied.

"Well, what we got to talk about that's so important that you approachin' me at my nephews' funeral?" Tee asked, stepping in between Proof and Mighty.

Moo said, "Look, I just wanna tell y'all we appreciate y'all allowing us to bury our loved one without no bullshit jumpin' off."

"Why you say that?" Zoo questioned.

"Fuck these Eastside ass niggas." Mighty scoffed, looking Moo up and down as he clutched his burner.

Tee said, "Be cool, Mighty. And y'all put that shit up! We at peace. Why wouldn't y'all be able to bury yours peacefully. Y'all ain't gotta worry about us, unless y'all break the truce you, your brother and Zoo agreed on."

"Worry?" Moo smirked.

U-Tee said, "Listen, right now it's all about my nephews and their buddies. I gotta figure out what happened with them. I heard about that young girl gettin' killed over there. Whoever the stupid muthafucka is that did it need to catch a few. I don't play when it comes to women and children."

"I agree," Moo said, looking at Proof, then Mighty.

Zoo said, "Our condolences on y'all loss."

"Same to y'all," Moo replied.

U-Tee tapped Zoo.

"Gotta go," Zoo said, as he turned and followed Tee toward the limos that awaited them.

Meanwhile, my mind was clicking as we walked back over to Autumn's service. I'd came to the conclusion that Zoo nor U-Tee had any idea Mighty and Proof were behind Autumn's death and Honesty being shot. That's why he hadn't sent a squad to retaliate. They didn't know 3C had killed U-Tee's nephews out of revenge. The look on the faces of the lil' niggas said it all though. They were guilty as sin and, they had to pay.

# Chapter 51

## *TELESIS*

### *Plottin'*

After everybody left the cemetery, we were all invited to the repast feast being held at Honesty and Autumn's grandmother's house. She owns a beautiful home out in Fox Point. Everything was being served, from turkey, ham, roast, greens, dressing, yams, macaroni, cornbread and chicken. They had mashed potatoes, gravy, cakes, pies and more. Honesty didn't have much of an appetite. She ain't do nothin' but pick over her food for the most part. She ate a lil' bit, just to make her granny smile.

Six was so bent on revenge, he didn't even attempt to eat. However, the rest of the crew had no problems digging in. Crook was on his third plate. For Six seeing all the photos of Autumn throughout the house was starting to get to him. He decided he needed some air. After seeing them niggaz at the burial grounds, I knew what was up. Six was plottin'.

I looked at Smoke, he looked at the squad. As if they'd read my mind, we all stood up and followed Six outside. Not being one to leave a plate unattended Crook asked Autumn's mother if it would be okay to take his plate outside. He promised to bring it back. She'd told him it was fine, and he caught up to us, plate in tow.

"I'm killin' them niggaz!" Six declared, pacing back in forth while puffing on a Newport. He was heated at the thought of being so close to the niggaz and not being able to touch 'em.

I was too! Smoke was trying to calm him down by assuring him that we'd get 'em. But he wasn't tryin' to hear that shit.

Six said, "Look, fuck talkin' about what we gon' do! These niggas still breathin', gettin' money and fuckin' bitches while we over here havin' Thanks Mutha-fuckin' Givin'!" He glanced at Crook, which sent all of our attention his way.

"What? I'm hungry!" Crook shrugged his shoulders. Feeling awkward as we all stared, he put his fried chicken leg back on the plate.

Six continued, "We just buried shorty! Honesty scarred for life, physically and mentally! Shits forever! Actions would feel a lot better than speakin' words, right now."

Tank said, "As bad as I want them dudes in the ground, we'll have to wait until the opportunity presents itself and take aim."

Bella said, "He's right. Right now, it's just too hot to ride down on 'em. Just give it a few weeks."

"A few weeks, huh?" he asked, taking another pull from his square.

Thirty said, "A few weeks is all we're askin'."

'Tank told him, "Honesty can't lose you to the system, right now. She needs you, and so do we."

Smoke said, "You know they gon' be on top of shit. They just lost five. We gotta be smarter than that."

I said, "Sixty days. In two months, we ride with or without 'em. You hear me, my dude?"

I walked over to him and hugged him. He knows, Honesty is my bitch! My heart. I told 'em, "In sixty days, we huntin' them niggas."

He rested his head on my shoulder and said, "In sixty, Lesis."

Crook said, "A'ight, y'all heard him! Sixty days. Now, let's go get some of that cheesecake. And, ooh, that German chocolate cake." He rubbed his hands together.

We all paused, and just looked at him. He always has a way of saying the stupidest shit at the most inappropriate times.

"Oops." He covered his mouth. "Did I say that out loud?" he had the nerve to ask, looking around.

We walked off on his dumb ass.

Smoke said, "Dog, you's a stupid muthafucka." He was shaking his head as we walked back toward the house.

To Be Continued…
The Streets Will Never Close 3
Coming Soon

**Lock Down Publications and Ca$h Presents** assisted publishing packages.

**BASIC PACKAGE** $499
Editing
Cover Design
Formatting

**UPGRADED PACKAGE** $800
Typing
Editing
Cover Design
Formatting

**ADVANCE PACKAGE** $1,200
Typing
Editing
Cover Design
Formatting
Copyright registration
Proofreading
Upload book to Amazon

**LDP SUPREME PACKAGE** $1,500
Typing
Editing
Cover Design
Formatting
Copyright registration
Proofreading
Set up Amazon account
Upload book to Amazon
Advertise on LDP Amazon and Facebook page

***Other services available upon request. Additional charges may apply

**Lock Down Publications**
**P.O. Box 944**
**Stockbridge, GA 30281-9998**
**Phone # 470 303-9761**

## Submission Guideline

Submit the first three chapters of your completed manuscript to ldpsubmissions@gmail.com, subject line: Your book's title. The manuscript must be in a .doc file and sent as an attachment. Document should be in Times New Roman, double spaced and in size 12 font. Also, provide your synopsis and full contact information. If sending multiple submissions, they must each be in a separate email.

Have a story but no way to send it electronically? You can still submit to LDP/Ca$h Presents. Send in the first three chapters, written or typed, of your completed manuscript to:

**LDP: Submissions Dept**
**Po Box 944**
**Stockbridge, Ga 30281**

*DO NOT send original manuscript. Must be a duplicate.*

Provide your synopsis and a cover letter containing your full contact information.

Thanks for considering LDP and Ca$h Presents.

**NEW RELEASES**

TOE TAGZ 4 by AH'MILLION
A GANGSTA'S QUR'AN 4 by ROMELL TUKES
THE COCAINE PRINCESS 2 by KING RIO
SAVAGE STORMS 3 by MEESHA
LOYAL TO THE SOIL 3 by JIBRIL WILLIAMS
THE STREETS WILL NEVER CLOSE by K'AJJI

**Coming Soon from Lock Down Publications/Ca$h Presents**

BLOOD OF A BOSS **VI**

SHADOWS OF THE GAME II

TRAP BASTARD II

By **Askari**

LOYAL TO THE GAME **IV**

By **T.J. & Jelissa**

IF TRUE SAVAGE **VIII**

MIDNIGHT CARTEL IV

DOPE BOY MAGIC IV

CITY OF KINGZ III

NIGHTMARE ON SILENT AVE II

THE PLUG OF LIL MEXICO II

By **Chris Green**

BLAST FOR ME **III**

A SAVAGE DOPEBOY III

CUTTHROAT MAFIA III

DUFFLE BAG CARTEL VII

HEARTLESS GOON VI

By **Ghost**

A HUSTLER'S DECEIT III

KILL ZONE II

BAE BELONGS TO ME III

By **Aryanna**

KING OF THE TRAP III

By **T.J. Edwards**

GORILLAZ IN THE BAY V

3X KRAZY III

STRAIGHT BEAST MODE II

**De'Kari**

KINGPIN KILLAZ IV

STREET KINGS III

PAID IN BLOOD III

CARTEL KILLAZ IV

DOPE GODS III

**Hood Rich**

SINS OF A HUSTLA II

**ASAD**

RICH $AVAGE II

MONEY IN THE GRAVE II

**By Martell Troublesome Bolden**

YAYO V

Bred In The Game 2

**S. Allen**

CREAM III

**By Yolanda Moore**

SON OF A DOPE FIEND III

HEAVEN GOT A GHETTO II

**By Renta**

LOYALTY AIN'T PROMISED III

**By Keith Williams**

I'M NOTHING WITHOUT HIS LOVE II

SINS OF A THUG II

TO THE THUG I LOVED BEFORE II

IN A HUSTLER I TRUST II

**By Monet Dragun**

QUIET MONEY IV

EXTENDED CLIP III

THUG LIFE IV

By **Trai'Quan**

THE STREETS MADE ME IV

By **Larry D. Wright**

IF YOU CROSS ME ONCE II

By **Anthony Fields**

THE STREETS WILL NEVER CLOSE III

**By K'ajji**

HARD AND RUTHLESS III

THE BILLIONAIRE BENTLEYS III

**Von Diesel**

KILLA KOUNTY III

**By Khufu**

MONEY GAME III

**By Smoove Dolla**

JACK BOYS VS DOPE BOYS II

A GANGSTA'S QUR'AN V

**By Romell Tukes**

MURDA WAS THE CASE II

**Elijah R. Freeman**

THE STREETS NEVER LET GO II

**By Robert Baptiste**

AN UNFORESEEN LOVE III

By **Meesha**

KING OF THE TRENCHES III
by **GHOST & TRANAY ADAMS**

MONEY MAFIA II

LOYAL TO THE SOIL III

By **Jibril Williams**

QUEEN OF THE ZOO II

By **Black Migo**

THE BRICK MAN IV

THE COCAINE PRINCESS III

**By King Rio**

VICIOUS LOYALTY II

**By Kingpen**

A GANGSTA'S PAIN II

**By J-Blunt**

CONFESSIONS OF A JACKBOY III

**By Nicholas Lock**

GRIMEY WAYS II

**By Ray Vinci**

KING KILLA II

**By Vincent "Vitto" Holloway**

## Available Now

RESTRAINING ORDER **I & II**

By **CA$H & Coffee**

LOVE KNOWS NO BOUNDARIES **I II & III**

By **Coffee**

RAISED AS A GOON I, II, III & IV

BRED BY THE SLUMS I, II, III

BLAST FOR ME I & II

ROTTEN TO THE CORE I II III

A BRONX TALE I, II, III

DUFFLE BAG CARTEL I II III IV V VI

HEARTLESS GOON I II III IV V

A SAVAGE DOPEBOY I II

DRUG LORDS I II III

CUTTHROAT MAFIA I II

KING OF THE TRENCHES

By **Ghost**

LAY IT DOWN **I & II**

LAST OF A DYING BREED I II

BLOOD STAINS OF A SHOTTA I & II III

By **Jamaica**

LOYAL TO THE GAME I II III

LIFE OF SIN I, II III

By **TJ & Jelissa**

BLOODY COMMAS I & II

SKI MASK CARTEL I  II & III

KING OF NEW YORK I II,III IV V

RISE TO POWER I II III

COKE KINGS I II III IV V

BORN HEARTLESS I II III IV

KING OF THE TRAP I II

By **T.J. Edwards**

IF LOVING HIM IS WRONG…I & II

LOVE ME EVEN WHEN IT HURTS I II III

By **Jelissa**

WHEN THE STREETS CLAP BACK I & II III

THE HEART OF A SAVAGE I II III

MONEY MAFIA

LOYAL TO THE SOIL I II

By **Jibril Williams**

A DISTINGUISHED THUG STOLE MY HEART I II & III

LOVE SHOULDN'T HURT I II III IV

RENEGADE BOYS I II III IV

PAID IN KARMA I II III

SAVAGE STORMS I II III

AN UNFORESEEN LOVE I II

By **Meesha**

A GANGSTER'S CODE I &, II III

A GANGSTER'S SYN I II III

THE SAVAGE LIFE I II III

CHAINED TO THE STREETS I II III

BLOOD ON THE MONEY I II III

A GANGSTA'S PAIN

**By J-Blunt**

PUSH IT TO THE LIMIT

By **Bre' Hayes**

BLOOD OF A BOSS **I, II, III, IV, V**

SHADOWS OF THE GAME

TRAP BASTARD

By **Askari**

THE STREETS BLEED MURDER **I, II & III**

THE HEART OF A GANGSTA I II& III

By **Jerry Jackson**

CUM FOR ME I II III IV V VI VII VIII

An **LDP Erotica Collaboration**

BRIDE OF A HUSTLA **I II & II**

THE FETTI GIRLS **I, II& III**

CORRUPTED BY A GANGSTA I, II III, IV

BLINDED BY HIS LOVE

THE PRICE YOU PAY FOR LOVE I, II ,III

DOPE GIRL MAGIC I II III

By **Destiny Skai**

WHEN A GOOD GIRL GOES BAD

By **Adrienne**

THE COST OF LOYALTY I II III

**By Kweli**

A GANGSTER'S REVENGE **I II III & IV**

THE BOSS MAN'S DAUGHTERS I II III IV V

A SAVAGE LOVE **I & II**

BAE BELONGS TO ME I II

A HUSTLER'S DECEIT I, II, III

WHAT BAD BITCHES DO I, II, III

SOUL OF A MONSTER I II III

KILL ZONE

A DOPE BOY'S QUEEN I II III

By **Aryanna**

A KINGPIN'S AMBITON

A KINGPIN'S AMBITION **II**

I MURDER FOR THE DOUGH

By **Ambitious**

TRUE SAVAGE I II III IV V VI VII

DOPE BOY MAGIC I, II, III

MIDNIGHT CARTEL I II III

CITY OF KINGZ I II

NIGHTMARE ON SILENT AVE

THE PLUG OF LIL MEXICO II

By **Chris Green**

A DOPEBOY'S PRAYER

By **Eddie "Wolf" Lee**

THE KING CARTEL **I, II & III**

By **Frank Gresham**

THESE NIGGAS AIN'T LOYAL **I, II & III**

By **Nikki Tee**

GANGSTA SHYT **I II &III**

By **CATO**

THE ULTIMATE BETRAYAL

By **Phoenix**

BOSS'N UP **I , II & III**

By **Royal Nicole**

I LOVE YOU TO DEATH

By **Destiny J**

I RIDE FOR MY HITTA

I STILL RIDE FOR MY HITTA

By **Misty Holt**

LOVE & CHASIN' PAPER

By **Qay Crockett**

TO DIE IN VAIN

SINS OF A HUSTLA

By **ASAD**

BROOKLYN HUSTLAZ

By **Boogsy Morina**

BROOKLYN ON LOCK I & II

By **Sonovia**

GANGSTA CITY

By **Teddy Duke**

A DRUG KING AND HIS DIAMOND I & II III

A DOPEMAN'S RICHES

HER MAN, MINE'S TOO I, II

CASH MONEY HO'S

THE WIFEY I USED TO BE I II

**By Nicole Goosby**

TRAPHOUSE KING **I II & III**

KINGPIN KILLAZ I II III

STREET KINGS I II

PAID IN BLOOD **I II**

CARTEL KILLAZ I II III

DOPE GODS I II

By **Hood Rich**

LIPSTICK KILLAH **I, II, III**

CRIME OF PASSION I II & III

FRIEND OR FOE I II III

By **Mimi**

STEADY MOBBN' **I, II, III**

THE STREETS STAINED MY SOUL I II III

By **Marcellus Allen**

WHO SHOT YA **I, II, III**

SON OF A DOPE FIEND I II

HEAVEN GOT A GHETTO

**Renta**

GORILLAZ IN THE BAY **I II III IV**

TEARS OF A GANGSTA I II

3X KRAZY I II

STRAIGHT BEAST MODE

**DE'KARI**

TRIGGADALE I II III

MURDAROBER WAS THE CASE

**Elijah R. Freeman**

GOD BLESS THE TRAPPERS I, II, III

THESE SCANDALOUS STREETS I, II, III

FEAR MY GANGSTA I, II, III IV, V

THESE STREETS DON'T LOVE NOBODY I, II

BURY ME A G I, II, III, IV, V

A GANGSTA'S EMPIRE I, II, III, IV

THE DOPEMAN'S BODYGAURD I II

THE REALEST KILLAZ I II III

THE LAST OF THE OGS I II III

**Tranay Adams**

THE STREETS ARE CALLING

**Duquie Wilson**

MARRIED TO A BOSS I II III

**By Destiny Skai & Chris Green**

KINGZ OF THE GAME I II III IV V VI

**Playa Ray**

SLAUGHTER GANG I II III

RUTHLESS HEART I II III

**By Willie Slaughter**

FUK SHYT

**By Blakk Diamond**

DON'T F#CK WITH MY HEART I II

**By Linnea**

ADDICTED TO THE DRAMA I II III

IN THE ARM OF HIS BOSS II

**By Jamila**

YAYO I II III IV

A SHOOTER'S AMBITION I II

BRED IN THE GAME

**By S. Allen**

TRAP GOD I II III

RICH $AVAGE

MONEY IN THE GRAVE I II

**By Martell Troublesome Bolden**

FOREVER GANGSTA

GLOCKS ON SATIN SHEETS I II

**By Adrian Dulan**

TOE TAGZ I II III IV

LEVELS TO THIS SHYT I II

**By Ah'Million**

KINGPIN DREAMS I II III

**By Paper Boi Rari**

CONFESSIONS OF A GANGSTA I II III IV

CONFESSIONS OF A JACKBOY I II

**By Nicholas Lock**

I'M NOTHING WITHOUT HIS LOVE

SINS OF A THUG

TO THE THUG I LOVED BEFORE

A GANGSTA SAVED XMAS

IN A HUSTLER I TRUST

**By Monet Dragun**

CAUGHT UP IN THE LIFE I II III

THE STREETS NEVER LET GO

**By Robert Baptiste**

NEW TO THE GAME I II III

MONEY, MURDER & MEMORIES I II III

By **Malik D. Rice**

LIFE OF A SAVAGE I II III

A GANGSTA'S QUR'AN I II III IV

MURDA SEASON I II III

GANGLAND CARTEL I II III

CHI'RAQ GANGSTAS I II III

KILLERS ON ELM STREET I II III

JACK BOYZ N DA BRONX I II III

A DOPEBOY'S DREAM I II III

JACK BOYS VS DOPE BOYS

By **Romell Tukes**

LOYALTY AIN'T PROMISED I II

**By Keith Williams**

QUIET MONEY I II III

THUG LIFE I II III

EXTENDED CLIP I II

By **Trai'Quan**

THE STREETS MADE ME I II III

By **Larry D. Wright**

THE ULTIMATE SACRIFICE I, II, III, IV, V, VI

KHADIFI

IF YOU CROSS ME ONCE

ANGEL I II

IN THE BLINK OF AN EYE

By **Anthony Fields**

THE LIFE OF A HOOD STAR

**By Ca$h & Rashia Wilson**

THE STREETS WILL NEVER CLOSE I II

**By K'ajji**

CREAM I II

**By Yolanda Moore**

NIGHTMARES OF A HUSTLA I II III

**By King Dream**

CONCRETE KILLA I II

VICIOUS LOYALTY

**By Kingpen**

HARD AND RUTHLESS I II

MOB TOWN 251

THE BILLIONAIRE BENTLEYS I II

**By Von Diesel**

GHOST MOB

**Stilloan Robinson**

MOB TIES I II III IV V

**By SayNoMore**

BODYMORE MURDERLAND I II III

**By Delmont Player**

FOR THE LOVE OF A BOSS

**By C. D. Blue**

MOBBED UP I II III IV

THE BRICK MAN I II III

THE COCAINE PRINCESS I II

**By King Rio**

KILLA KOUNTY I II

**By Khufu**

MONEY GAME I II

**By Smoove Dolla**

A GANGSTA'S KARMA I II

**By FLAME**

KING OF THE TRENCHES I II

by **GHOST & TRANAY ADAMS**

QUEEN OF THE ZOO

By **Black Migo**

GRIMEY WAYS

**By Ray Vinci**

XMAS WITH AN ATL SHOOTER

**By Ca$h & Destiny Skai**

KING KILLA

**By Vincent "Vitto" Holloway**

**BOOKS BY LDP'S CEO, CA$H**

TRUST IN NO MAN

TRUST IN NO MAN 2

TRUST IN NO MAN 3

BONDED BY BLOOD

SHORTY GOT A THUG

THUGS CRY

THUGS CRY 2

THUGS CRY 3

TRUST NO BITCH

TRUST NO BITCH 2

TRUST NO BITCH 3

TIL MY CASKET DROPS

RESTRAINING ORDER

RESTRAINING ORDER 2

IN LOVE WITH A CONVICT

LIFE OF A HOOD STAR

XMAS WITH AN ATL SHOOTER

KING KILLA

**By Vincent "Vitto" Holloway**

**BOOKS BY LDP'S CEO, CA$H**

TRUST IN NO MAN

TRUST IN NO MAN 2

TRUST IN NO MAN 3

BONDED BY BLOOD

SHORTY GOT A THUG

THUGS CRY

THUGS CRY 2

THUGS CRY 3

TRUST NO BITCH

TRUST NO BITCH 2

TRUST NO BITCH 3

TIL MY CASKET DROPS

RESTRAINING ORDER

RESTRAINING ORDER 2

IN LOVE WITH A CONVICT

LIFE OF A HOOD STAR

XMAS WITH AN ATL SHOOTER

www.ingramcontent.com/pod-product-compliance
Lightning Source LLC
LaVergne TN
LVHW010057110826
845155LV00028B/380

* 9 7 8 1 9 5 5 2 7 0 6 2 5 *